REVIEW

OVE CONQUERS ALL. HAVE YOU ever wondered why bad things happen? What good could possibly come when bad things occur? "Hard to say I'm Sorry" is a wonderful love story about just that. The authors have captured the emotions, drama, and suspense of those who are going through the "bad"...and with God's help, coming out of the other side, back to love. Get ready for one of the best love stories in a long time.

—Cheryl LeBarre, Akron East High School. Class of 1983

DEDICATION

IN THE COURSE OF CONCLUDING the final chapters of "Hard to Say I'm Sorry," my partner, Leslie A. Matheny, strongly suggested this book be dedicated to those men and women who served our country over the years. The novel truly encapsulates the struggles soldiers of war face.

While most Americans applaud and appreciate the services of these young men and women, many people do no understand the physical, psychological, and emotional struggles they endure upon returning home. They never realize that there are more casualties to war than those whose lives end on some foreign soil. Those who return home must suffer the harsh realities of war and the guilt that is sometimes associated for returning to the states alive where they could finish their lives with their families and friends.

INTRODUCTION

T HROUGHOUT THE SCRIPTURES, THERE IS an underlying theme that resonates from the book of Genesis to the final chapters of Revelation. It is the idea of forgiveness. Throughout the ages, God has sought to restore mankind to an active relationship with Him. In the Old Testament, He chose the children of Israel to promote this message of repentance and reconciliation. And as the Old Testament tells time and time again, the children of Israel failed miserably to proclaim the Grace so desperately desired to shower upon the world.

In the New Testament, God takes another step forward. He sends forth His only begotten Son to demonstrate the true extent of His love for the world. From the moment His Son is conceived to the time He is crucified, readers discover God's true and tender heart for a lost people. Yet, like the Old Testament, people have a hard time accepting the simple fact that God desires to have an open and working relationship with them: especially in light of the wrongs that have been recorded throughout history.

Forgiveness is the key to freedom. It is what unlocks the soul from bondage of the past only to breath new live into the present. It is something that most people never truly experience. I could offer several explanations as to what prevent people from seeking true redemption, yet there is one that stands out above all. That is, the heart. Yes, the heart.

For centuries, people have been told a lie. From the moment they learn the difference between right and wrong, children are constantly bombarded with this concept of change. That is, in order for them to be restored to their original favor with family and friends, they must do something in order to receive approval. While there is truth in this teaching, God shares how He "loved the world so much that He gave His only begotten Son (John 3:16). In other words, His Son paid the penalty for the trespasses committed against a Holy God: a righteous God.

All God requires is that a person believes in His word. That's it. Belief is a powerful thing. When and if a person can fully comprehend and believe forgiveness is contingent on his or her faith in Christ (Ephesians 2:8-9) then he or she would be saved.

"Hard to Say I'm Sorry" is premised on this concept. A young mercenary finds himself struggling with not only his past but also his present. He falls in love, and in the process he continually seeks to make amends for the wrongs he committed. He is haunted between the two extremes: his past and his present.

He struggles to believe that someone could honestly fall in love with him regardless of his so-called crimes. In his journey to redemption, he learns there is more to love than what appears on the surface: it is something that dwells deep within the soul. It is not until he comes to the ultimate test that he learns the true meaning of forgiveness.

And in the end, he returns to the place that plagued his spirit for so long, only to discover the true meaning of letting go as well as what it means to love and to be loved.

Chapter 1

"THE MISSION"

I T WAS NOVEMBER 26, 1984. A "band of brothers," as they were called, quietly crossed the borders of Honduras. With the new moon, this evening was particularly darker than most. The temperature hovered near 80 degrees. The air was heavy with humidity. With clear skies, the stars were their only source of light.

The mission for this "band of brothers," ten in total, was to infiltrate a warehouse where marijuana and munitions were stored. According to intelligence reports, this mission was to be swift and simple. Because the storage facility was located in one of the most rugged terrain, the intelligence report read the grounds were not heavily fortified.

To avoid any type of detection, these ten men hiked the rugged hills of the Honduras landscape. In the cover of darkness, with only the stars to guide them, this "band of brothers" scaled down some of the steepest slopes; they crossed a swift flowing stream, and made their ascent on the other side of the mountainous terrain.

They mustered just outside the camp. The lights overlooking the grounds beamed brightly. As was reported, there appeared to be no activity on the grounds. Each man went over the strategies laid out for him. Some were to set trip mines outside the compound perimeters, while others were instructed to torch the warehouse to the ground. Nothing was to be salvaged from this sanctuary for sinners.

After synchronizing their watches, each man was supposed to muster at a point where two helicopters were waiting. Initially, everything went without incident. Some men were outside setting booby traps, others silently cut through the steel fencing and started to slowly crawl to the infrastructure soon to be deemed unsuitable.

What happened next was by no means anticipated. One of the men accidentally crept over a sensor, signaling the presence of intruders. A fortress considered unoccupied was anything but. As soon as the sensor shot off its signal, the storehouse doors flung open.

A hail of gunfire soon replaced the silence of that evening. The stars that once illuminated the night sky were drowned by the sea of smoke from below. Every man was in for the fight of his life. Those skirting the perimeter quickly came to offer support to those trapped within the barrage of bullets. Their blood that evening stained the earth's soil. There was no helping them. There was no judge or jury to condemn or convict. They were sentenced as their lifeless bodies lay.

Those still outside of the fence scattered. In the midst of all the mayhem, they became disoriented and disbanded. They lost their bearings. Two of the men teamed up. Of the "band of brothers," they were like brothers. They did their training together, as well as perform other missions.

They very well understood the risks. They knew there might come a day when they would meet their maker. But, they were young men and ambitious to serve their country.

During training, they made a pact with one another. The promise was that neither one would allow the other to be caught behind enemy lines. Never did they ever believe they would have to serve their papers to the other.

Unfortunately, though, in their haste to vacate the premises, the one just happened to get tangled in a trip mine. In as soon as his boot snapped the line, the explosion was immediate. His body flew through the air as if being tossed like a rag doll. His legs were blown up and out. As the result of the shrapnel, his bowels were exposed to the outside elements.

On that foreign land and under the stars that once again started to glisten, he cried out for his mother and to meet his maker. His brother quickly turned to the point of impact. There he found his other half in half. His brother's face was laced with horror. Panic and pain had set in. Lying on the ground, he looked his partner in the eyes and pleaded that he make good on their promise.

His brother fell to knees. "I can't!" He shouted. He then held the head of the fellow soldier as if he were cradling a baby. "I can't! Please don't make me do it" He repeated out loud.

"You must!" His brother struggled to say. "You can't let them find me like this." He took a deep breath to spit out: "You know they are going to kill me anyway." But that was not the only thing he spit. Blood started to fill first his lungs and then his lips.

There is one thing their training did not teach: it's the ability to eradicate the conscience. Sobbing bitterly, his friend reached his right hand down to the knife nestled comfortably on his belt. He unclasped the strap that held the sharp object snugly to his side. He raised the knife and placed it against his brother's neck.

Still cradling his wounded brother's head with his left hand, the young soldier begged for forgiveness. "Just, do it!" The paralyzed soldier cried.

The young soldier proceeded to swipe the blade left to right across the injured soldier's neck. He could feel the blood of his brother begin to drip from the knife's tip, down its spine, onto its handle and then off its pommel. The blood made it difficult for him to maintain a handle on his weapon. It slipped from his grasp and fell to the ground.

He jumped to his feet. Shock started to set in. He looked up to determine his location by the stars. His attempts were interrupted. One of the guards from the storehouse heard the commotion between the two soldiers. It was not difficult for him to sneak up on the standing soldier as he gazed upon the heavens.

He grabbed the soldier from behind and shouted: "Te voy a matar:" which means: "I am going to kill you." The young soldier could feel the strength of the guard's hands. He could literally feel the life being squeezed out of him.

His training kicked in. He cocked his right elbow and struck a backward blow into the guard's abdomen. He did so with such force the guard had no choice but to free his grip on the young soldier.

The two men then squared off and faced one another. The young soldier understood the gravity of the situation. The guard was much larger and stronger than he. He knew there was not going to be a happy ending for one of them. He prayed that he was not the one. The guard threw a punch wide right.

The soldier quickly ducked, picked up the knife he'd dropped a few moments ago, and with one swift thrust, he stabbed the guard on the left side. It found its desired target underneath the guard's rib cage. For the second time within a matter of moments, blood steadily streamed down from the knife's blade.

The soldier looked the guard in the eyes. Fear is what he witnessed. The guard was mortally wounded. He would be dead within moments. His eyes bulged from his face as his breathing became labored. He started to cough up blood. The smell was horrid and horrific.

With adrenaline working in favor of the young soldier, he returned the same words the guard sputtered: "Te voy a matar!" To emphasize his point, the soldier twisted his blade in the guard's chest cavity where it now rested before he withdrew it. The guard, in turn, spewed up some more blood: upon such time his body went limp and fell lifelessly to the ground.

The young soldier could hear others scour the grounds. He started to run down the ravine from which he climbed earlier. To deter any possibility that his scent may be traced and tracked, the soldier sprinted to a stream that parted the hills. The current was swift and strong. To make matters worse, the stream was paved with rocks: some rocks were smooth and slippery; while others were sharp and serrated. His body was growing weak and weary. His legs were starting to wane on him as he high-stepped down stream.

Believing he had run far enough to distract his pursuers, the young soldier found refuge against a large tree. What he believed to be a haven of rest ended up being a place of remorse. Unbeknownst to the young soldier, he had camped on top of a nest of "bullet ants."

The "bullet ant" is an indigenous insect in Central America. Its sting is ranked to be the most powerful among insects. If stung, the victim is known to experience intense and extreme neurological pain for up to 24 hours.

This soldier planted and pitted himself in a position of unspeakable odds. If he screamed from the army of ants as they marched up his body casting their campaign of constant stings, then he would give away his location. If he remained silent, then he would have to endure the merciless massacre of ants. Either situation yielded the same result. To refrain from giving up his position, he ripped off a piece of clothing from his blood soaked uniform and bit into it until his body succumbed to the pain. He became unconscious.

Some villagers found him some days later. They were making their way to the stream for water when they found him lying next to the tree. The ants retreated once the threat no longer presented itself. The villagers were not sure what to do.

News about the failed mission swept through the villages. They received reports that some soldiers made it out alive. They were also reminded to report any stranger to the authorities in the event any stranger or soldier was seen. A word of warning was tagged with any sightings of the renegades: to aid and assist any foreign person meant certain death. Initially, they decided to leave him lay. They did not want to be seen caring for what was described as the enemy. Yet, they did not want to support the drug activity that was polluting the hearts and minds of their people as well.

They reported their findings to their village chief. It was thus decided that action would be taken at dusk. The chances of being seen were greatly diminished as the new moon was beginning to break into a crescent.

When the sun started to settle behind the mountains, a team was escorted to the body. Remarkably, the young soldier was still alive. They, with the utmost expediency, raised his limp body from the ground and rushed him to the village. Ladies were summoned to tend to the countless number of bites that seemed to become one with his body. Cold compresses were continually placed on him. There was a 24-hour vigil over him.

Because of dehydration, the ladies forced liquids down his throat. After several days, he awakened from his sleep. The officials wasted no time in notifying the U. S. Embassy. Though the United States Government denied all claims of any involvement in such a debauchery, they did not hesitate to send representatives to retrieve survivors.

He was taken to a secure facility in Central America. There he was interrogated for days about the misfortunes of that evening. Under the intensity of lights, he was demoralized, depersonalized, debriefed and desensitized.

The government he so faithfully served denied him. They betrayed him along with those who lost their lives as well as the other three who made it out alive. Sure, each man went into each mission knowing the risks. That was one thing. It is another thing when a mission fails because of false intelligence. It was a difficult pill to swallow.

Eventually, this young soldier, along with the other three, was released and freed to return home. They were given strict orders never to share the episode that occurred on that November evening in 1984 in the hills of Honduras.

Chapter 2

"MANSLAUGHTER UNDER THE MOONLIGHT"

DESPITE THE GOVERNMENT'S BEST EFFORTS to debrief and desensitized this young soldier, it failed to erase all memories of that night long ago. Occasionally, he would wake up drenched in sweat, yelling out commands, crying, and stabbing his pillow. He could not shake the nightmares of seeing the faces of dying people, nor could he overcome the sensation of having died somewhere.

There were certain things that served as triggers. The sights and sounds of fireworks sent shivers down his spine. He took cover the moment a truck backfired. People who spoke Spanish seemed to instill this insatiable anger that needed to be quenched.

So it was one evening as he joined some friends at a local establishment. They went to watch the Cleveland Indians take on the New York Yankees to win a spot in the World Series. At that time, it was considered one of the best playoff games in the history of the Major League Baseball. The Indians dethroned the Yankees in seven games.

But like most sporting events, alcohol was the beverage of choice. Everyone seemed to be enjoying this game of the century, while enjoying a brew or two.

At a table sitting next to them were the rivals. It was a group of men rooting for the opposing team. "How could they? How dare they sit in Cleveland country and root for the Yankees" The gibbering and jabbering went on throughout the game. At first, it was playful. However, with each beer bottle being passed from one person to the next, things became as heated in the establishment as it did on the field.

Afterwards, some threats were made. Most people thought they were nothing more than verbal enticements from one table to the next. They thought wrong. Their verbal assaults rattled the soldier of old. They reminded him of a threat long ago.

It just so happened that his eye caught a gentleman sitting quietly at the other table. He remained neutral throughout the encounter and exchange of words. He would have nothing to do with it. From the conversation, the soldier gathered that the gentleman was a happily married man with a two-year old daughter at home.

If anything, it was he who tried to extinguish the fire between the two camps. All he desired to do was spend some time with friends and return to his family. Fate was not on his side.

Walking to his car, he was greeted by the young soldier. The full moon illuminated the night sky. Everything was calm outside: outside of a gentle breeze blowing.

There was nothing to alarm either one of any impending danger. The young soldier just wanted to have a final jab or two in the spirit of friendly rivalry. Jokingly, he said: "That's right, man! Get in your car and head back to New York from where you came."

Jokingly and unknowingly, the gentleman was about to pull a trigger on the young man. Yes, he was originally from New York. As such, he spoke Spanish as fluently as he did English.

He smiled only to say: "Te amo:" which means: "I love you."

In as soon as the wounded soldier heard the words, he went on the defensive. Something snapped in his memory. His mind traveled down memory lane and before he knew it, he was standing before his enemy.

"What did you tell me?" He demanded to know.

"Nothing!" the man politely replied. "Forget, I said anything!"

"I don't think so!" The young soldier snapped. "You just threatened to kill me, didn't you?"

"No! I didn't" Realizing that he was completely misunderstood, the man tried to recant. He repeated the phrase again: "Te amo." Before he could say anything else, the soldier's mind went blank. When he came to, he found the man lying on the ground. His larynx was crushed. The man pled for help but there was no help to get. Everyone else remained in the bar to celebrate the Indians victory over the Yanks.

The soldier's mind was caught between two worlds: his past and now his present. Acting like a soldier of old, he did an about-face and walked away. He was completely oblivious as to what transpired. In his mind, he served his country. In stride and in cadence with each step, the young soldier returned to what he believed was his barracks.

It was not until he heard the news the following morning that he became cognizant of what happened the night before. For some strange reason, he felt responsible for what happened.

Chapter 3

"THE KNOCK ON THE DOOR"

G RACE PUT THE BABY TO bed hours ago. Even though Rosie was two years old, Grace still referred to her as the baby. It was late and despite her best efforts, Grace was having a hard time keeping her eyes open. She was expecting a phone call from Ray, her husband who was in Cleveland, Ohio with friends for the Indians and Yankees showdown.

Ray and Grace lived in Jamestown, NY. He was a pilot in the US Air National Guard stationed in Jamestown, NY. Grace was a city employee who worked on the Park and Recreation Board.

Ray had been home for a few months. He was sent to Grenada when Operation Fury began. When the mission ended, he remained deployed to the Caribbean for an additional six months on a peacekeeping mission

Ray missed one too many evenings away from Grace and Rosie. While he was looking forward to the big game in Cleveland with a few of his fellow soldiers, his buddies secured a hotel for the evening, but Ray wanted to return home after the game. David, one of Ray's Guard buddies had a friend that owned an eatery in downtown Cleveland. He invited David to bring a few of his friends over to watch the game in his pub.

Before leaving Jamestown and heading for Cleveland, Ray gave Grace and Rosie a hug and a kiss. He told them he would see them later that evening. He promised to call before he got on the road. Grace would know after his phone call, her husband would be home an hour and a half later.

Grace focused on the sound of the pendulum swinging back and forth. As the clock ticked away, Grace started to worry. Trying to dismiss her uneasy feeling, she figured that Ray must have drank too much. He knew better. He would not drive home. "But why hasn't he called?" she wondered. She picked up the phone to listen for a dial tone.

Unable to keep her eyes open, she fell asleep. The last thing she remembered was looking at the clock. It read 1:35 a.m.

Loud knocking woke Grace from her slumber. She looked at Ray's pillow. She could tell that he had not been home. She looked at the clock; 4:08 a.m. Sliding out of bed, "Big dummy must have forgotten his key," she said to herself.

She looked through the peephole. Instant panic struck when she saw that it was not her husband, but rather an official military vehicle parked in the street. Two dressed officials were standing at her door. Grace knew the news would not be good.

Her knees buckled and her entire body shook as she turned the opened the door. "Grace Howard?" The man with the glasses asked.

With tears rolling down her cheek, "What happened?" She asked with a voice quivering.

"There was an altercation in Cleveland, Ohio that involved your husband. He was killed Ma'am. Police found his military I.D. card and called us. His body is en route to the Jamestown Armory as we speak. There will be an investigation by Cleveland P.D." Handing Grace a card, the officer with the glasses said. "This is the name and phone number of the detective assigned to the case. Sorry for your loss Ma'am." And with that, the two soldiers walked back to their vehicle.

Chapter 4

"The Love of My Life"

G RACE AND RAY HOWARD BOTH grew up on the Fort
Drum Army Base in Jefferson County, New York.
Ray was a few years older than she. Their paths
crossed on base, but they didn't run around with the same
group of people. Ray knew that once he was old enough, he
would enlist and live his adult life in the military. Grace, on
the other hand, could not wait to turn eighteen and venture
off on her own living the life of a civilian. She had enough of
the military lifestyle.

She watched the devastation her mother went through
every time her father was deployed. The tearful goodbyes and
the restless nights were too much. Grace also hated the way
her father would return from his missions: moody, irritable,
crazy at times. Grace also hated living on an Army base. She
wanted to experience the freedom of civilian life.

After graduating from high school, she and her best
friend Liz rented a small house in Jamestown, New York
where she enrolled in Jamestown Community College. One
day on campus, Grace spied Ray. He was standing behind a
booth passing out National Guard pamphlets. She had not

seen him for several years, but she recognized him from their time at Fort Drum.

She thought Ray looked quite handsome in his uniform. She wondered if he would remember her. As she approached him, she could tell by his huge smile that he recognized her right away. Striking up a conversation, they hit it off. Ray invited Grace for dinner and the rest was history

Coming from a military childhood, Grace fit right in with Ray's National Guard family. It was through the wife of one of Ray's battalion members, that she found her job in the Jamestown Park and Recreation Bureau.

After a year-long romance, Ray popped the question and she accepted. They were married in a traditional Catholic ceremony. More so than a wedding, the church resembled a formal military gathering. Ray was well loved by his Guard family. The little kids of his Guard friends affectionately called him Uncle Ray. He went out of his way to make those around him feel loved, wanted, and appreciated.

Ray had experienced war and the sorrow that comes with it. His mantra was to make everyone feel like they were special. He witnessed too many innocent people suffer. While Grace was not crazy about going back to living a military lifestyle, she loved Ray and would go wherever life would take them.

Ray and Grace were blessed with a supportive family, a wonderful extended family, and careers they both loved. Their blessings grew when Grace found out she was pregnant. She was ecstatic and could not wait to become a mother.

On the day she was to tell Ray, he unexpectedly for no reason at all, showed up at home with six red roses. "If the baby is a girl, her name will be Rose." It was a sign.

And now Grace's perfect life came crashing to a halt. Raymond was gone and her life was left in shambles. She collapsed into a chair, bawling in disbelief.

She would have to pull herself together to be strong for Rose. She had phone calls to make but it was only 5:00 in the morning. Wanting to be at the Armory when Ray's body arrived, Grace called her mom.

Chapter 5

"The Road to Repentance"

J AMES WAS BESIDE HIMSELF AS details of Ray's death came to light. Everything about his encounter with Ray was a blur. All James could remember was watching the game with some friends. When Ray's picture flashed across the screen, James recognized him. He remembered Ray sitting at a table in the proximity of his. He faintly recalled shouting some superlative's at Ray's companions as they were in waters well over their heads.

He recalled thinking: "Who in their right mind would dare enter Cleveland territory only to root for an opposing team?" He had yet to make the connection between him and his altercation with Ray. It was not until the phone rang that light was shed on James involvement.

His friend Larry was watching the same news as James. Larry could not believe that a murder occurred outside the establishment where they teamed up to cheer and, then, to celebrate. "Did you hear what happened last night?" he asked.

Still trying to make sense out of this nonsense, James answered: "Yes. Yes, I did! I am watching the news as we speak."

Larry then said something that forced James to realize his possible involvement as to what took place. He asked: "Did you see anything peculiar in the parking lot? You did leave approximately the same time as the man killed."

There was a long pause at the other end of the line.

"James, are you there?" Larry inquired. "Did you by chance see anything?"

Struggling to answer Larry's question, James was slow to answer. "Could I be the one responsible for taking the life of this husband and father?" he asked to himself.

"James, are you okay?" Larry would not let the topic go. "You did see something, didn't you?" he added. "You need to notify the police about what you saw and heard. Did you know he was part of the U.S. Air National Guard?"

"No, I didn't." James said.

"Which question are you answering?" Larry continued to probe. "No, you didn't see or hear anything, or you did not know he was part of the military?"

Seeing Larry had given him a back door pass, James seized it. "Both!" he said agitated. "I did not see or hear anything and no, I did not know he was part of the Armed Forces."

Sensing James irritation to the interrogation, Larry discontinued his line of questioning. "Okay, I am just asking." If anyone knew about James past, it was Larry. They had been friends since they were in elementary school. James confided in Larry regarding everything. Yet, despite Larry's knowledge of James history, never in a million years would he have thought James was somehow involved.

"Look, Larry." James said trying to end their conversation. "It was a long and late evening. I am running late for work. I need to let you go."

Though Larry knew that James did not work on Sunday's, he attributed James' response to too much celebrating. Fearful that James' mood would only intensify, Larry was not about to question him any further.

Larry concluded their conversation with: "Well, when you can call me?" He went so far as to change the topic entirely. "Remember." Larry said enthusiastically. "We have a championship next week. We are playing in the World Series. I can't wait. Maybe this will be the year," he concluded

"Yeah!" James said half-heartedly. "We will make plans to watch the game together. Maybe this week, we'll watch it at my place. You know there is a murderer on the loose?"

"That's a great idea. I will call the other guys. You furnish the pizza and we will bring the appetizers. I will talk to you later."

The line on Larry's end went dead. James could not help but listen to the flat-line on the receiver, reminding him that a man's heart flat-lined the night before. For some strange reason, he had some part in what happened.

He looked at his watch. It was still early. James walked to his sleeping quarters, sat on the edge of his bed. He placed his head in the cup of his hands and started to cry. "What have I done? What am I to do?"

His heart was heavy. It was void. To think that another man's life ended by his hands. The bedroom clock showed 09:00. Most churches started their services at 10:30. He still had plenty of time get ready to attend a Sunday morning service.

Nervously, he showered and shaved. Every part of his body trembled. He threw on the best scrubs he could muster from his closet and then went in search of a church. He drove aimlessly through the streets of Cleveland. Every church he drove past either seemed too stoic or too simple and small. In either case, they did not seem suitable to handle his sins.

With the former, James sensed he would be criticized and condemned. In the latter scenario, he surmised that his problems were too large for a church whose main sanctuary was only seen from a storefront window. He was soon to give up. That is, until he found a church nestled in the center of a neighborhood hidden by the commercialism that lined the main drag of a community on the outskirts of town.

It was larger than most of the churches he passed that morning. As a visitor, James could easily get lost in the crowd of people who came to congregant. He entered its threshold where he was cordially greeted. An usher walked James to an empty seat.

Everything about the morning service seemed to speak to him: the worship, the music, but more importantly the message. It inspired James. The pastor was seasoned. He was prolific in speech, but what even impressed him more was how the pastor believed in what he preached.

Of all the messages to hear on that particular morning and under those particular circumstances, the sermon centered on "repentance." The pastor focused his message on the words of the Apostle Paul. It was his letter to the church of Corinth. In it, Paul reminded his readers of the new life given to those who call upon the Lord.

In the fifth chapter of II Corinthians, starting with verse 17, Paul penned these words: "Therefore if any man be in Christ, he is a new creature: old things are passed away; behold all things become new (NKJV)" Those words jump-started a heart that had died some years ago.

James clearly understood what he must do. He must become a new creature: he must become a new creation. That day he repented for all he had done and for all that he had become. And in the end, he was a new creation. And from that point on, he reasoned in his mind to do everything he could do to rectify his wrongs.

He would start with helping a woman who lost her husband and a daughter grieving the loss of her father. The task, he knew, would be difficult, but not insurmountable. God had given him a clean heart and a new purpose.

Chapter 6

"BIG CHANGES"

G RACE PULLED HERSELF TOGETHER AND phoned her mother. Her parents would have a five-hour drive ahead of them. She called her sister in Norfolk. And then she called Ray's mother. His father had passed away earlier in the year. His mother moved south to a condo community where Ray's Aunt Mary lived.

Grace wanted to speak with Jason and David: Ray's closest Guard buddies that had gone to the game with him. She would have to wait until they were back in Jamestown to find out what happened.

Grace called the number for Detective Callahan; he had very little information for her. "Passersby found your husband on the ground next to his car. He had already expired. It didn't appear to be a robbery. No witnesses have come forward and nobody reported any kind of altercation last night. We will continue to investigate."

She told Detective Callahan that her husband had been with friends that night. She gave him the phone numbers for Jason and David. She told him they stayed the night somewhere in Cleveland. Ray decided to drive home instead.

"I'll be in touch." he said, and then he hung up.

When Rosie woke up, Grace told her the heartbreaking news. Rose was young enough that the poignant conversation between mother and daughter was hard for her to comprehend. Grace was thankful that her daughter would not have to deal with the gut wrenching loss, but it also deeply troubled her that Rose would not remember her father.

She pulled out a notebook from the desk and jotted down her thoughts. One way to keep the memory of Raymond alive would be to write a daily journal entry. She would hand the journals over to Rose when she was older.

As the morning progressed, the news spread through the Jamestown National Guard family. The phone calls poured in. Neighbors and friends were descending upon the house like a swarm of paratroopers dropping from the sky.

When her parents arrived, they headed over to the Armory. Grace was permitted time with her husband's body, but the others would have to wait until the calling hours.

The next few days were a blur as she made the final arrangements for her husband. It was difficult for the Command Sergeant Major to see his little girl hurting. He vowed to do whatever necessary to find the person responsible for the murder of his son-in-law.

"How ironic that Ray was murdered in a restaurant parking lot," Grace thought to herself. In spite of her sadness, she laughed a little thinking of all the time she spent worrying about him while out in combat.

Chapter 7

"A Friend at a Funeral"

J AMES CLOSELY FOLLOWED THE NEWS of Ray's murder. He happened to catch wind when and where the memorial service was to take place. That morning, James walked into his supervisor's office and respectfully requested to take some days off. He worked for an independent energy company. They were responsible for restoring downed lines after severe storms.

His supervisor sensed that James was troubled. He asked: "James is everything okay?"

"No Sir." James replied. He went on about how he felt led to attend the funeral of the person killed in the parking lot of a nearby establishment.

The supervisor was somewhat shocked. Believing that James and Ray were close friends, his supervisor was sympathetic to James' request. "I'm so sorry James. I didn't know you knew him. By all means, your request is granted. And James, if there is anything I can do to help, by all means ask me."

"Thank you, sir." James replied. He walked out numb. Never did he want to give his supervisor the false impression that he and Ray were friends. But, at the same time, he did not want to give any indication that he might be involved in his murder.

That evening, James started to pack his suitcase. He knew he had to do something about his appearance. Over the years, he abandoned the military look for a more modern look. He grew a beard and mustache that resembled a wild brush in some remote woods. He even went so far as to allow his hair to grow past his ears and down his neck.

He opened up a bathroom cabinet and pulled out "Old Faithful:" his electric razor. He proceeded to shave: "High and tight!" That's what they used to say. "High and tight!" he chuckled.

When all was said and done, James looked ten years younger and he could pass for a person serving in the military. He liked what he saw. It had been a long time. But there was one thing he could not replace: his eyes. Since his time in Honduras, they were never the same. They showed no form of life. They were the portals to his soul where only death was welcomed.

Morning quickly came. James hit the floor at precisely 0500. As in years past, he returned to his former days as a soldier. He got squared away in a matter of moments before he took to the open road.

His mind wondered about so many things. "Am I doing the right thing?" "Should I turn myself in?" "What do I say to the wife and his daughter?" Such thoughts swirled around the vast region known as the conscience. Regardless, he stayed true to his mission. He kept his sights on the road and headed to the service.

"No turning back, soldier!" he reminded himself. "You have a mission, now complete it."

Finally, he reached his destination: "Point Charlie!" He decided to call it. The line for those waiting to offer their condolences was long. The service was to begin within an hour. Believing he would not have the chance to speak to Ray's wife, James almost turned his car around

But James found himself being pulled from his vehicle only to take his place in line. He stood silent. He listened to everything everyone was saying regarding Ray. There was so much he learned as he politely listened. Then again, he was trained to become familiar with his surroundings. He was an expert in waiting, watching, and working through the most difficult situations.

With moments to spare, James made it to Grace and Rosie. Initially, it was difficult for him to look into the face of this widow and her daughter. However, James felt compelled. He felt driven. He looked up only to be completely swept off his feet.

She was stunning. She had long dark hair that was pulled up to accentuate the beauty of her neckline. Her eyes were as blue as the ocean and her smile had the power and potential to blind a person. It was her strength, by far, that James found most appealing. She handled herself well given the circumstances: the circumstances he created.

"I'm… I'm sorry for your loss, ma'am." James said. He looked down to be equally captivated by Rosie. She reminded James of a doll a person would find on display in a toy store window.

Grace responded with grace. "Were you a friend of Ray's?"

One thing James learned during his training was deception. Never give the enemy more information than what was required. Clearly, Grace was not an enemy, but James had to be careful what he said and how he said it. Listening to everyone in line, there was one thing he discovered. He and Ray served during the same time. That was the card he played.

"Ma'am, your husband and I served our country at the same time." James answered.

James did not lose his touch. His skill worked. He deliberately led Grace to believe he and Ray served together.

"Oh! I know how Ray was fond of all his friends: especially those he served with."

James literally got away with murder. He stood in disbelief. He came to offer his comfort to the wife he made into a widow only to be comforted by this widow who was once a wife.

"Ma'am," James softly spoke. "I want you to know I will do whatever I can to help you. If it is okay, may we remain in touch?"

Though Grace found his request somewhat awkward, she understood that many people made similar requests. She also understood that while most people's intentions were noble, the majority of them would never follow through with them.

"I would greatly appreciate that!" she said. "Could you please remind me of your name, again?"

"It is James, ma'am. James McIntyre."

"Well, James McIntyre, please call me Grace; Grace Howard."

"Thank you. I will be in touch. I must be going now." James informed her.

"James. Thank you!" Grace had opened the door to James heart. He had made a friend.

Chapter 8

"A Beautiful Morning for a Burial"

RAY WAS BURIED THE FOLLOWING morning. The October air was crisp but the sun was out. The morning was beautiful. In the cemetery, Grace could not concentrate on the priest; she was taking in the beauty surrounding her.

A beautiful blue sky above; the aroma of fresh fallen leaves hung in the air. The leaves were putting on a show with their colors of red, orange, and yellow. If there were such a thing, it was a beautiful morning for a burial.

While Ray's showing was a large public affair, the burial in the cemetery was small and private. Family and a few of their closest friends surrounded Grace and Rosie.

When the graveside service was over, Grace's parents headed back to Fort Drum, taking Rosie with them. "Gracie honey, let us take the baby for a few days. You take care of yourself and let us take care of Rosie."

Grace bid farewell to Ray's mother, and then dropped her sister off at the airport before heading home.

Pulling into her driveway, Grace stared at the house. She didn't want to remain there without Ray. They bought the house together. It was once a place of great joy, and now it was a place of great sadness. Instead of rushing through the door, excited to see her family, she now dreaded walking through the threshold of an empty house. "It's a house." she thought. "It is no longer a home."

Once inside, she phoned Detective Callahan. There was no change in the case. She then set about finding the paper work regarding military death benefits and life insurance claims. She wasn't sure if she would be able to afford the house without her husband's income. She wasn't even sure she wanted to keep that house. "Ray, send me a sign. I don't know what I'm supposed to do."

Feeling overwhelmed, Grace succumbed to the beauty of the fall day. She pulled her bicycle from the garage and headed to the Allegheny State Park. On her ride, Grace thought back on the many friends that called on Ray. "James," she said aloud. She pictured him in her mind. "He seemed very distraught."

Locking her bike to a tree, she headed towards the river. She sat on the bank and stared blankly into the water. The Chadakoin River was not a large river; it was more like a small stream. But it was a good place to sit and clear one's mind. A man sitting along the bank a little further down caught her attention. Not wanting to be rude by staring, she thought it might be James. She only saw him for a brief moment earlier in the morning, but it sure looked like him. "Oh crap!" Feeling embarrassed, Grace gave a polite wave when the man on the bank caught her gazing toward him.

Chapter 9

"A Walker or a Stalker"

GRACE WAS A BIT AT ease to discover that it was James sitting a stone throw's away. "How ironic is that?" she thought. "What are the chances of a chance encounter: especially on this particular path and by the side of this stream."

"James! What are you doing here?" she asked.

Any doubts written across her mind were quickly erased. James was quite forthright with her "I drove by your house when I saw you on your bike. Concerned about your well-being, I thought it best to follow you."

"How many men would even take the time?" she reasoned. "Besides, it was not like he tried to be covert."

Politely, James squatted and then sat next to her. The steady flow of the stream was soothing. Maybe, it was a little too soothing. The sound of the water as it washed over stones and stirring silt from its surface, took James to a different time. A time he had long forgotten.

She could not help but notice how his mind had drifted as quickly as the water drifted downstream. "James," she interrupted. "Are you okay?"

Immediately, his mind snapped to the present. "Yes, Grace. Thank you." he said. "There is something about rushing water that makes my mind follow its course downstream. Sounds crazy, doesn't it?"

"No. No it doesn't." she laughed. "I understand exactly what you mean. You just never know what path a stream may take."

Gaining confidence in him, Grace asked a simple yet powerful question: "How long did you know Ray?"

He was not quite prepared for that question and paused for a second or two. "Answer the question as it is asked." he thought. "Well, Grace. I did not know him for very long. In fact, our encounter with one another was by chance. But it is what I remember about him that is important."

"And what was it that made such an impression on you." Grace had to know.

"Well. It is not too often you meet a man who is devoted to both his country and his family." Referring to the night of his death, James added: "I remember how he wanted so desperately to return home to his wife and daughter."

Grace was moved by his words. She believed him to refer to his time overseas. If there was one thing James learned during his time of service: it was the art of deception.

"Look, it is starting to get dark. Please, let me drive you home."

"What about my bike?" Grace inquired.

"Oh! We can put it in the back of my car. I have a bike rack to set it on."

Questioned asked and answered. But there was one question Grace did not ask. It was so obvious; it was overlooked. She failed to ask James this one simple and pertinent question: "How did you know where I lived?"

Chapter 10

"Men of Honor"

R AY AND GRACE HAD A zest for life. They both took risks. They were daredevils of sorts. They were very much grounded in three important elements: faith, family, and friends. If James dared to call himself a friend of Ray's, she knew that he had to be a man of honor. Ray would not befriend a person with little integrity.

"So James, tell me; Ray had his own greeting that he used when he came across a brother. Are you familiar with his greeting?" She knew that if James was indeed a friend, he would know Raymond's greeting.

The wheels in his mind started to spin. "What was it he said to me in the parking lot that night?" James tried to remember. "Te amo." he replied.

"Yep, that is it," she said with a smile on her face. "Ray spent time in Corpus Christi working in the helicopter depot. He traveled back and forth through Central America so often that it forced him to master his ability to speak fluent Spanish."

Grace thought it was nice to have a conversation with someone who didn't have the look of pity in his eyes. Jason and David couldn't face Grace during Ray's services. They both felt guilty for what had happened after the game. She cried with them. She told them it was not their fault. She absorbed their pain and hoped they would find release from feeling responsible.

She still was not sure what to make of James. He seemed nice enough. He did not come across as a threat. She thought he was 'a nice guy'.

En route to her house, Grace spouted off driving directions as they conversed. She could not believe how she made herself so vulnerable to a man she just met. But there was something about James that started to play on the strings of her already fragile heart. "Was it his stature or was it that he took the time to care?" she was not sure.

Pulling into the driveway, James got out and removed her bike from the back of his car. "I hate to trouble you anymore this evening," she said. "But would you mind taking a look at this crazy paperwork I have to fill out? The wording on it is confusing and I suppose I need to get it turned in before I take off."

Raising his eyebrows, James asked. "Oh! Where are you going?"

"I am heading to Cleveland, Ohio." she replied. "I have to see where it happened."

Chapter 11

"From the Interstate to the Interrogation Room"

J AMES COULD NOT BELIEVE HIS ears. "You are going to Cleveland?"

"Yes." Grace responded. "I know it sounds crazy, but I do need closure. I need to see where Raymond took his last breath."

Sympathetic to her grief, James was cognizant of closure. Quickly, he offered his services once again. "I live in Cleveland. I was going to return in the morning. Would you like for me to drive you there?"

She was somewhat shocked. "You drove to New York to attend Raymond's funeral?" she inquired. Yet her apprehensions were dismissed when she thought about all the people Raymond influenced. Many servicemen and women traveled across the country to attend his service.

"What should make James any different?" she wondered. "Sure, they barely knew one another, but that was Raymond. He touched so many lives in so many different ways."

"How would I return home?" she queried.

"I will be more than happy to drive you back home."
James said confidently. "Shall I pick you up around 0700?"

After a brief meditation and reflection, she accepted his
offer. "Can you have me home by the weekend?"

"It will be no problem. I will have you home whenever
you are ready to return. And by all means, please tell your
parents. I do not want them to worry about their daughter."

Whatever doubts she had regarding James were removed.
He seemed genuine about her safety, so much so that he gave
her personal information to share with her parents.

That morning, he was as prompt as usual and was
sitting outside her driveway. He bent over backwards to
demonstrate his loyalty to Raymond, but more importantly,
to Raymond's family.

Grace struggled to get her keys in the lock to secure her
front door. She was carrying a suitcase, her purse, and a few
other personal things. She was rattled and rightfully so. After
all, she was traveling with practically a stranger to the site her
husband died.

James got out of the car. He took the case Grace
desperately tried to handle and carried it to his car. He then
went so far as to open the passenger door for her.

"Are you sure this is what you want to do?" he asked.

"No, no I am not." she said sorrowfully. "It is something
I need to do."

With those final parting words, James backed out of her
driveway and started their drive to Cleveland. There was very
little conversation between them. He knew this was going
to be just as much difficult for her as it was for him. By all
means, he clearly understood she was sitting next to the man
responsible for taking her husband's life.

Upon entering Cleveland and prior to taking Grace to
a nearby Marriott, he did ask if he could stop by his place.

Hoping she would accept his invitation to lunch, he needed to stop by his place to grab some extra cash. She graciously accepted his request to take this short detour.

Much to their dismay, Detective Callahan greeted them in the parking lot. He was leaning against the driver's side of his car when James pulled in. He approached James with caution. Handing James his card, "I'm Detective Callahan." he said. "I'm investigating a homicide." He was both polite and professional. "Sir, you need to come to the station with me."

James was bewildered. "May I ask for what purpose?"

Detective Callahan refused to give any details. "Sir, we can either do this the easy way or the hard way. It is your choice."

Still confused, James went to bat for Grace. "With all due respect, detective, may I have the privilege of at least taking this young lady to her hotel?"

"I am afraid not." Detective Callahan sternly said. "I will make sure she will find a hotel nearby."

Grace was dumbfounded. "Detective Callahan? I am Grace Howard from Jamestown, New York. You are investigating the murder of my husband Ray! What is this all about?"

"Ma'am, we have a few questions for your friend. That's all," he said.

"Oh my goodness!" Grace shouted. "You do not think he has anything to do with my husband's murder?" She then countered her own question with a question. "Or do you?"

"Ma'am, all I can say is that bar patrons saw this gentleman in the establishment that evening."

"Is that true, James?" she demanded an answer.

James came clean. "Yes, yes it is. I saw Raymond. He was sitting at the table next to us."

Wanting to know more, Grace did an interrogation of her own. "And you were planning to tell me this vital piece of information when?"

Both the Detective and Grace could see how deeply sorrowful James was regarding what happened to Raymond henceforth.

Sobbing somewhat bitterly, James responded with an answer that seemed to appease the detective and Grace. "Had I known his life was in peril, I would have done everything I could to save him. Ironically, we caught up on some old business in the men's room as we did our business." James elaborated. "Raymond stood to his left, only to say those two words he was notorious for: 'Te amo."

James then went on to add that he almost missed his desired target when he heard Raymond's salutation. There was only one person he ever knew who greeted his friend in such fashion. James shared how Raymond discussed his desire to return home to his wife and daughter after the game. To add emphasis, James stated: "That was a typical Raymond respond. Faith, family, and friends were always important."

Referring to his time in Honduras, his next remark was heartfelt. "I failed him. I could not save a fellow soldier. For that, there is no forgiveness."

Looking into Grace's deep blue eyes, he added: "How do I say I'm sorry? A fellow soldier died on my watch. That is unacceptable. It is unforgivable. If I could have done anything to change the outcome, believe me, I would have."

Detective Callahan, seasoned in the field of murders, sensed the sincerity of James' words. The interrogation planned at police headquarters was postponed. You cannot fake the type of remorse James demonstrated. Surprisingly,

Detective Callahan gave James a free pass. "I can call you if I have any further questions?"

"Yes sir! I would be more than happy to help in this investigation." James said both assuredly and remorsefully.

Chapter 12

"A Decline to Dinner"

SO MANY THINGS WERE RUNNING through Grace's mind. "I have spoken on the phone with Detective Callahan. This was certainly a weird way of meeting him," Grace said to James. She could not shake a feeling of uneasiness that had descended upon her. "How freaking odd?"

"What's that?" James asked. Not realizing she spoke out loud: "Oh, there are just too many strange things regarding Ray's murder. It just seems weird to me: nothing seems to be adding up," she replied.

She took a good hard look at James and couldn't decide if he was a friend or a foe. She thought back to a conversation she had with herself. She did ask Ray to send her a sign. Was James the sign?

Rethinking lunch, Grace changed her mind. Not being familiar with the city, she said to James, "Please drop me off at a hotel within walking distance to the restaurant where Ray was killed."

She wondered if Ray's car would still be in the parking lot. With the commotion of the last few days, his car was the last thing on her mind. She would be sure to call the detective and ask about it.

James took her to the Marriott and helped her settle in. She told him that she planned to walk over to the stadium and then to the Clevelander Bar and Grill later that evening.

"Would you like for me to accompany you?" James asked.

"No thanks," she replied. "I would like to go alone. But if I'm not intruding," she added, "Would you like to meet me for dinner later tonight? It has been a rough few days and I enjoy your company."

"What time would you like for me to pick you up?" James asked.

"I should be ready around six," she suggested.

"Then six it will be," he graciously affirmed.

"I will be waiting for you under the carport." Grace softly spoke. She knew this afternoon was going to be difficult. She went to the stadium. She could not believe her husband was killed over nothing more than a baseball game. Cleveland already had a bad reputation for its unruly and unsportsmanlike behavior. But what happened to Raymond crossed the line. It went well beyond the parameters: It was an inside pitch that spun out of control.

From the stadium, she slowly walked back to the Marriott. She could not help but think of Raymond's final moments. "What were his thoughts before he drew his last breath?" she wondered. "Was he thinking of his family? Was it worth it?"

Her mind ran a continuous marathon of thoughts. She was exhausted by the time she made it to the Marriott and decided to hold off going to the bar's parking lot.

She went to her room and dropped dead to the world. Her dreams were interrupted by the thoughts that raced through her mind. The alarm she set to chime at 5:00 p.m. sounded off. She was slow to crawl out bed. But she knew James would be waiting. She went into the bathroom, took a hot shower and then prepared herself for what was to come.

James was sitting outside when she came down from her room. As a gentleman, James was standing outside of the car. He stood by the passenger side door and opened it as she approached.

"Where would you like to go for dinner?" he asked.

He was not prepared for Grace's answer. "Please take me to the place where Raymond's life ended."

Sympathetic to her condition, James asked: "Grace. Are you sure this is what you really want?" He was not sure who was going to have a more difficult surveying the scene: he or Grace?

With Cleveland still buzzing over their victory from the week prior, traffic was exceptionally busy. People in Cleveland had high hopes. This was the year. Grace could not understand how people cared more for a sports team than a man murdered because of that team.

Eventually they made it to the bar and grill. The parking lot was packed. The only parking space available was unavailable. A yellow tape protected its perimeters: it clearly read: "Crime Scene." Raymond's car was towed earlier that week for processing.

James slowly rolled up to the space that once had an occupant. "James, can you please stop?" Grace tearfully requested.

Not wanting to look suspicious of his involvement in Raymond's death, James parked the car. He started to get out with Grace but she put the brakes on his kind gesture. "I need some time alone."

"I understand," James replied. In so many ways he was thankful. He could not bear the thought of standing on such "hallowed ground." As she walked to the vacant plot, his mind went back to the evening in question. His only recollection of the sequence of events was fuzzy at best. All he could recall was Raymond's infamous salutation: "Te amo."

Grace stood in silence. The tears she held back for so long started to steadily flow down her cheeks. She grabbed a tissue in an attempt to dam the water, but to no avail. Once her tears broke through the watertight integrity doors, there was no stopping them.

A gentle breeze blew across the parking lot. From underneath a nearby car, a piece of paper that once lay comfortably beneath a vehicle was awakened. It blew in the air only to land in front of Grace. Though her eyes were drenched with tears, it caught her attention. She bent over and picked it up.

It was a carbon copy credit card stub from the night Raymond was killed. Remarkably, Grace could make out the first name of the person who signed for the bill. It read: "Larry." At the time, Grace did not think much about the significance of this vital piece of evidence. She folded the tab in half and placed it in the pocket of her jacket.

She did an about-face and returned to the car. "What did you find?" James asked.

"Oh, it was nothing but a piece of paper blowing in the wind."

To continue to cover his tracks, James remained calm, cool, and collective. He had to ask though everything about him begged him not to: "Did you want to go inside?" He feared that he would be recognized by some of the staff regarding the night in question.

Thankfully, Grace declined. "No, I have seen enough. If you don't mind, could you please take me back to my hotel?"

James breathed a sigh of relief. "Yes, I can." He chauffeured Grace back to the Marriott. The ride was solemn. He could see the hurt in Grace's blue eyes. He could not help but think that he was the source of that hurt.

Chapter 13

"Standing Guard"

G RACE'S HEART WAS BOMBARDED WITH every possible emotion imaginable. The reality of Raymond's death started to set in. James looked to his right only to see her distress. He witnessed that same look time and time again. The human mind can only tackle so much in a given period of time before it needs to leave the field of play and to sit the bench.

James pulled the car into one of the parking spaces at the Marriott. Grace glanced over and asked rather harshly: "What do you think you are doing?"

"I am going to walk you to your room," he said. It was not so much what he said; it was how he said it. It was a direct command. Living with Raymond, Grace learned that tone all too well.

"I beg your pardon?" she snapped. "Don't you dare talk to me as if I am a soldier?"

"My apologies ma'am, I want to make sure you make it to your room safely." James calm demeanor diminished any doubt Grace had. She knew deep in her heart that the walls around her were starting to shrink. She felt smothered. She was suffocating with grief.

They exited the car. James made sure he stayed by Grace's side. She was quite shaken and he feared that she might faint. And faint, she did. The elevator stopped on the second floor. Fumbling to get her key in the lock, everything started to spin. She collapsed and James was there to catch her in his arms.

Carrying her, James made up his mind not to leave. He would stand guard. Never will he ever leave another soldier behind enemy lines. Holding onto Grace with one arm, he struggled to place her key card in the door.

Taking the key from Grace, James got the door opened. He used his elbow to flip the switch on the entry light. He handled her as if she was a valuable piece of art. He gently laid her on one side of the bed. He then unfolded the covers on the other side of the mattress only to comfortably wrap Grace beneath the comforter.

He then pulled up one of the chairs and positioned it next to her. James sat there watching over Grace. He stood guard. Every now and then she would whimper in her sleep. At such times, James would take his fingers and run them through her long brown hair assuring her that everything was okay.

In so doing, James could not help but think of the fateful night where he cupped his best friend's head with his hands. He wept standing guard and Grace whimpered as she slept.

Chapter 14

"Dead Men Tell Tales"

U PON AWAKENING, GRACE WAS DISORIENTED for a brief moment. She laid there staring at the clock on the nightstand. It flashed 8:10 p.m. Her stomach growled. Rolling over onto her back, she let out a scream when she saw James sitting in a chair. Her scream startled James, who then bolted from his chair.

With her adrenaline pumping and her voice hoarse, "You scared the crap out of me. I didn't realize you were still here." Grace felt comfort in seeing James upon awakening, but quickly dismissed the feeling.

Standing in front of the large picture window with the lights of the city illuminating behind him, James could have easily been mistaken for an angel.

With that thought, she remembered bits and pieces of the dream she had while napping. In her dream, Ray had come to her and told her that James was safe. His orders were very direct to Grace: "Let James care for you and Rosie. He is the good guy."

"Grace, are you alright?" James asked.

Snapping back to the present, Grace said, "Yes, I was just remembering my dream. It was about you." James could sense a smile on Grace's heart.

Chapter 15

"Dust in the Wind"

THE TIME SPENT WITH GRACE stirred emotions that James had long forgotten. She made him feel alive. Returning home, James walked into his apartment and checked his answering machine.

There were several messages. All of them were from Larry. With each passing message, he could hear Larry's agitation.

"James!" Larry said in one recording. "Where are you man? Remember, we were to meet at your place for the first game of the World Series. You were so to supply the pizza! Call me when you get this!"

Another message became somewhat alarming to James. "Come on man! Where are you? Man you can't drop us like this! Call me or I might have to seriously hurt you."

Taken aback by the last message, James picked up his phone to call Larry. James was never one to leave business unsettled. Larry was right. They did make plans to watch the game at his place. But his absence that weekend did not warrant such an outburst or a threat.

The phone rang, but there was no answer on the other end. James would leave a message, but Larry never thought it was important to purchase an answering machine. But then again, Larry was known for owing every type of creditor on the market.

He hung up the phone, only to be rudely interrupted by Larry busting through his door. "Where have you been?" Larry shouted. "You let us down!"

Initially, James thought Larry was acting like a "drama king."

"Come on man, there are seven games in a series," James tried to explain. "I will make it up with you the next one."

There was something remarkably different about James' facial expressions as well as the way he handled himself physically. Larry picked up on it almost immediately. "What's going on? You have changed. I can tell."

Larry started to laugh. "Oh! I see. You finally found yourself a woman. Didn't you?" he inquired. "You can tell me, man."

"Well, I suppose I did, sort of," James said smiling.

"This is going to be good." Larry wanted so desperately to know who could have the digs on his buddy of old. "Who is she? Do I know her?"

James was not quite sure how to start or how much he should share with his buddy. "Well?" James started to spit out.

"Well, what?" Larry begged.

"Do you remember that man killed in the parking lot?" James asked.

"Yeah, what about him?" Larry's demeanor started to change. "Don't tell me you and his wife started hitting it off?"

"Not exactly," James stated. "I felt obligated to help her out. You know, she lost her husband and her daughter is now without a father."

"Are you out of your mind?" Larry demanded. "What are trying to do: get us into trouble?"

"I am trying to help her out, dude. Relax." James smiled as he thought about Grace. "By the way, how am I going to get us into trouble?"

"Do I have to draw you a map?" Larry said sarcastically. "Don't you remember soldier boy?"

James had a look of confusion about him. Sure, there were little snippets of that evening he remembered. But what happened in the parking lot was nothing more than a blur: a bad dream.

Larry shook his head in disgust. "Let me shake your memory. He and his 'little buddies' sat next to us. We had an exchange of words as they came onto our turf to cheer on the Yankees."

"So? How is that going to get us into trouble?"

"You are so stupid! I am sick and tired of you always using your past as an excuse."

Jokingly, James added fuel to the flames already burning in Larry's furnace. "For heaven's sake, man, you make it sound like we had something to do with his death."

"I'm done with you James. I am telling you, she is bad news for us, man." Larry followed his statement with a warning. "Go ahead! Keep it up. I promise you will eventually be behind bars."

"Is that a threat?" James laughed. "And don't you dare tell me what I should or should not do. I am a grown man."

Shrugging his shoulders, Larry had enough. "That's fine. You do whatever you need to do. For me, you are nothing but dust in the wind. Say your goodbyes, because you will never see me again."

From the time they were childhood pals, Larry always declared their friendship to be over. James could not count the numerous times Larry made that stupid comment: "You are nothing but dust in the wind."

He laughed as he watched Larry leave. "I'll see you soon. And when I do, I'll have a dust pan!"

Chapter 16

"LOVE BLOSSOMS"

OVER THE NEXT YEAR JAMES spent much time with Grace and Rosie. Military gossip spread through the city of Jamestown that Grace had moved on too soon; but she and James were nothing more than friends. She paid no mind to the gossip.

Shortly after Ray's death, Grace decided to sell the house that she and Raymond bought together. There were too many painful memories. It was their dream to build their lives together as well as their family. As fate would have it, their dreams died when Raymond died. Her house sold very quickly. She opted to move closer to her parents in Jefferson County by Fort Drum. James enjoyed helping Grace find the perfect house for her and Rosie.

During the year following Ray's death, James and Grace grew closer. They spoke almost every night on the phone. They logged many miles traveling back and forth between Cleveland and Fort Drum. Shortly after Grace moved away from Jamestown, James relocated near Fort Drum to be closer to Grace and her family. A relationship that started out as a stranger at a funeral a year prior was changing; at least for Grace it was.

After James moved to New York, he and Grace were together most evenings. It was not unusual to find James at Grace's place.

Grace laid Rosie to bed and joined James on the porch swing. It was a chilly fall night. Grace loved this time of the year. The aroma of a bon fire lingered in the air. Lit pumpkins grinned with crooked smiles. The night could not be more perfect.

A shiver gave Grace goose bumps.

"Would you like me to grab your jacket?" James asked.

"Just say it Grace. Tell him." she thought to herself. "Just say the words." She scooted over as close to him as she could possibly get. "Your arms are all I need to keep me warm." She laid her head on his shoulder and drew a heart on his pant leg with her finger. "I'm in love with you James. I am totally and completely in love you with."

Expressing her feelings for James felt like a weight had been lifted from her shoulders. She wondered if he would reciprocate the sentiment, or if she would scare him off.

Chapter 17

"A SEASONED SOLDIER GOT OFF-GUARD"

GRACE'S WORDS CAUGHT JAMES COMPLETELY off-guard. He had grown affectionate toward Grace and Rosie. Over the past year, they had become such an integral and inseparable part of his life. He could not picture his life without them. He came to appreciate the love Raymond had for his family. And yes, he felt the same way toward Grace as she did him.

James had a difficult time digesting the fact that someone could fall in love with him. He wondered whether Grace would have the same feelings for him had she known the past that continued to haunt him in his dreams and, the fact, that he may have been responsible for Raymond's death. He accepted her invitation to draw closer, but was somewhat aloof to verbalize any type of expression.

While they snuggled, Grace sensed that James emotionally distanced himself from her. Somewhat shocked, Grace placed her right hand on his cheek, only to direct his eyes towards hers. There was something quite distinct about his eyes. They were void of life. She then knew that James bore the brunt of his past. What that past entailed, she did not know. But there was one thing for certain: she had fallen for this fallen soldier of the past.

And if her words did not catch this soldier off-guard, her next course of actions did. Grace took the initiative. She ran her right hand behind James' neck only to guide his face ever so close to hers. Before finishing her bold action of pressing her lips to his, she softly whispered the same words she did some moments ago: "I'm in love with you James." With that, their lips touched for the very first time.

He could feel her passion. Her kiss resuscitated the life that once ended in the hills of Honduras. Afterwards, she pulled away only to look in his eyes a second time. This time, she believed, to see life restored to them. They lit up. There were now signs of life.

Not being the romantic, James embraced Grace with so much passion that she knew he shared the same feelings toward her as she did him. James confirmed her dream where Raymond encouraged her to move on with life with the man she had fallen for. That evening, in the stillness of the evening and on the solitude of a swing, a romance was born.

James smiled. "I have one favor to ask you Grace?" He said so tenderly.

"What is that?"

"Please, I beg you." James heartily laughed. "Please never catch me off-guard like that again."

"Why, Mr. James. I never thought that was possible."

Chapter 18

"What Will the Future Hold?"

TUCKED UNDER A BLANKET SNUGGLED on the swing, Grace was content. Her parents were fond of James. Rosie adored him. She loved him. Ray approved.

Grace was lost in thought, daydreaming of what could be. She did not want James to go home that night. She imagined being a family with James as the head. She always considered herself strong and independent, but she liked the feeling of leaning on James. His strength made her feel secure and she liked it.

Grace recognized the gift she had been given. Not only was she fortunate to have found love with Ray, but she also found it again with James. Unlike Ray, who was vibrant and outgoing, James was quiet; a man of few words. Grace was drawn to him. It was his piercing eyes and strong jaw line that drew her in. He mesmerized her. He was brawny and tough. Under his strapping façade, she hoped she would find a mushy romantic and she believed she had.

"If I could stop time, I would stop it right now." Grace thought to herself. She did not want the evening to end. With work in the morning, she knew James would be heading home soon.

Grace's heart was racing. She had not been with a man since Ray, and she wanted James. "James, will you stay the night?"

Chapter 19

"A Case So Close to Going Cold"

THE ROMANTIC EVENING CAME TO a crashing halt. The phone rang. Grace questioned who would call her at such an hour. It was Detective Callahan. There really was nothing substantial pertaining to Raymond's death. Several leads were carefully investigated. Unfortunately, though, they led to nothing but dead ends. Raymond's case was on the verge of joining the already growing number of "Cold Case" files.

Unbelievably, the Homicide Unit received a promising lead. It was from a patron who witnessed the bantering and bashing between the two tables. This person had information that could not be ignored. He had too many details. One of which pertained to James.

According to this person's recollection, James was seen leaving at approximately the same time as Raymond. The informant went a step further. He saw James approaching Raymond. At the time of their altercation, James' was described as being "highly irritated."

Detective Callahan heard the same rumors that others helped spread. He was very much aware that Grace and James had built a relationship. And like most people, he even believed that Grace and James friendship advanced rather rapidly. To further his suspicions, he knew that many people have died for a lot less.

He asked Grace if James could be found on her premises. She was not one to lie. The evidence, while compelling, was more than circumstantial. In the past year, she, unlike most people saw something in James. He was a caring and compassionate man.

James had never given her any reason to doubt him or his deep desire to be a friend. "You are barking up the wrong tree." Grace insisted. "James is innocent."

"I understand your concern, Grace." Detective Callahan persisted. "But the evidence is both overwhelming and compelling. May I speak with him?"

Grace reluctantly summoned James to the phone. "Hello." He answered.

"James, some light has been shed over the death of Raymond." The detective explained. "We received word that you may know more about what happened than you initially led me to believe."

"Oh!" James said reservedly. "Is it something that can be discussed over the phone?"

"I am afraid it isn't." The Detective noted. "We really do need for you to return to Cleveland and clarify a few points of interest."

Sweat started to drench his face. How he dealt with this situation would define the direction of both the investigation as well as his vested interested in Grace.

James was trained to answer questions when asked. He refused to open any more doors than the ones already opened.

Maintaining his composure, he assured the detective that he would be at the police station by noon. After all, he figured this time would eventually come. He also said he would do anything and everything to help with the investigation.

He finished his conversation with the Detective. Grace could not believe everything that happened. She shared her most intimate feelings with James: only to discover that he knew more than what he led others on to believe. For all she knew, James could have been the man who murdered her husband.

"Well?" Grace demanded to know. She was perturbed and had every right to be. "Is it true? Do you know more about that happened that night than what you told me?"

"Grace. I know this does not sound good and, by all means, and it probably looks a lot worse." James said. "But I have been honest in all my answers. I wish I could tell you more, but I can't."

She looked into James' eyes. He was being truthful. He was being honest. She wanted to believe him. In fact, she did believe. She tried to reason. "Whoever said something to Detective Callahan: and whatever that person said must be a big misunderstanding."

"Hopefully, I can settle and subdue any suspensions tomorrow." James added. For some odd and strange reason, James was well aware that his meeting at the police station was going to be intense. In fact, it was going to be a full-fledge interrogation. It was nothing he had not experienced before.

"Everything will work out," James said.

Chapter 20

"The Long and Winding Road"

Before heading back to Cleveland, James went to Rosie's room where he kissed her on the cheek. "I'll be back, sweetie. I promise." He whispered in her ear. Rosie smiled as she slept so peacefully.

James started to make his way to his car. Grace was by his side. "I believe in you James," She confidently proclaimed.

Grace was shocked when James embraced her and did something very atypical. He cried. "James, what's wrong? Why are you crying?"

"I wish I knew." He sobbed bitterly. "I just don't know how to say I'm sorry…"

"Sorry for what?" Grace took a step back. She used her long fingers to wipe the tears from his face.

"I just don't know." James continued. "It seems that anytime I get too close to anyone, that person is snatched away from me."

"Honey! What are you talking about? Who?" Grace's curiosity started to peek. "Are you holding something back from me James?"

"I can't! I just can't!" he sounded off.

Trying to maintain her composure, Grace started to show signs of irritability. "You can't what? I can't help you, if you don't open up to me!"

"No! No! No! If I did, there is no way you could ever love me! Grace, Grace, I gotta go!"

James pecked her on the cheek only to get in his car. He left her standing. Disappointment would be an understatement. Grace was beyond disappointed. "What is he not telling me?" she wondered as she stared off in disbelief.

Watching him drive away in the darkness of night, there was nothing she could to do, or was there? She made up her mind that night not to let James down. She would meet him in Cleveland the following day.

James, on the other hand, could not control the tears that naturally flowed from his tear ducts. On several occasions James pounded his steering wheel in frustration.

Unbeknownst to him, he experienced several triggers that brought his past to the forefront of his subconscious. Unbelievably, it started on the swing. To have someone articulate the words "I love you," was comforting yet confusing. He couldn't comprehend why anyone could love him: why anyone would love him. "Had she known?" James continued to repeat over and over again.

His apprehensions were heightened by the phone call from the Detective: the thought of being interrogated, and let's not forget, there was a new moon out that evening. The stars were sparkling high about the atmosphere. A gentle breeze blew north to south. Everything brought him back to that long a winding road of so many years ago.

Driving became extremely difficult. With the torrential rainfall occurring behind the steering wheel, James pulled his car to the side of the road. He got out hoping to collect his thoughts: the sound of a babbling stream drew him in.

He had to hurdle the guardrail and double-timed down the wooded embankment to the stream. At its most outer edge, he fell to his knees and looked up into the sky. His mind was in another place and at another time. "Why?" He shouted out. "Why?"

Out of nowhere, he heard a voice. "Why? What?" Startled, James stood tall and turned to the sound of the voice. It was the friend he had left behind in Honduras.

James couldn't believe what he was seeing. "Markland? Is that you?" James exclaimed. "It can't be."

"Well buddy, it is."

There was something strikingly different about Markland. The last time James saw him; the lower half of Markland's body was blown to pieces. It was by James' hand that Markland drew his last breath. But now, Markland's disheveled body was restored: it was renewed. There was a certain aura about and around him.

In somewhat of a state of shock, James spoke to his old friend. "I thought you were dead? How can this be?"

"Remember, you idiot, you just asked for me?" Markland echoed. "You know, there were times you could be such a ditz. Did I ever tell you that?"

"No!" James answered and then asked. "Really?"

"Oh man! For being such a brave and brilliant soldier, you still have a lot to learn." Markland laughed and then countered with a question that went against all logic. "You want to know how is it that your life was spared and mine was slain."

"Yes. I need to know!" James wept uncontrollably. "You were like a brother to me. I didn't want to do what I did."

"James, you did what I begged you to do. It's not your fault." Markland reminded him. "And besides, it was my time and not yours. You know the Good Book says: 'For there is a time for every purpose and for every work. (Ecclesiastes 3:17: NKVJ).'"

Markland continued on: "Now soldier quit crying like a baby! There is another battle that needs to be fought and another battle for you to win. Go and fight like you were trained to!"

James went to hug his brother. Unfortunately, he was standing on an anthill. He aroused its occupants from their hibernation. Before he knew it, they were marching up his pant leg. A few had already started their strike by biting him. James looked down to swat them away. When he returned to his vertical position, Markland had disappeared or dissipated.

"Thank you!" James cried as he looked into the heavens. "Thank you!" He rushed up the ravine, returned to his car and made his route to Cleveland. To occupy his mind and his time, he turned on his radio. As fate would have it, the song playing across the airwaves was none other than the Beatles: The Long and Winding Road."

Chapter 21

"Someone's Knocking at Your Heart."

TRYING TO MAKE SENSE OF the evening, Grace pulled her wedding album out of a bureau. She sat at the kitchen table looking at pictures from one of the happiest days of her life. She shuddered at the thought that James was somehow involved in Ray's death.

She thumbed her way through the journals she kept since Ray's death as well. The journals were a road map of sorts leading Grace down the trail leading to James' heart.

Waves of foolishness passed through her. "Was the past year a set up?" she wondered. She anguished over the decision to drive to Cleveland to support the man she just professed her love for. It was a seven-hour drive. She would have to make her mind up; and fast.

Dialing the phone, "Hi Mom, sorry it's so late. Can I talk to Dad?" Now crying, "Dad, I need your help." After speaking with her father, Grace felt more at ease. He reassured her that he had James investigated shortly after he first came on the scene.

"He checked out. Everything he claimed to be and the places he claimed to have gone were all true."

James had no reason to lie. Grace had dated some real duds before meeting and marrying Ray. She thought she was pretty good at reading people. There was nothing about James that sent up a red flag.

Dialing the phone once more, "Hi Dad," before Grace could say anything more, her dad interrupted; "Be at the airstrip by 0700 and your mother said to drop Rosie at the house on your way."

"Thanks Dad, I love you so much!" Grace said as she hung up the phone.

Grace got very little sleep that night. Her mind wandered in all sorts of directions. When she tried to be mad at James, her heart wouldn't let her. She mourned for Ray, but looked forward to building a new life with a man she had fallen in love with. Her heart and her mind were being pulled in too many directions.

When morning rolled around, Grace called her boss and asked for a few days off to take care of business related to the murder. She packed a bag for Rosie, who was now awake and excited to spend a day or two with Grandma and Grandpa. Grace hastily tossed a bag together and headed to her parent's house.

Touching down in Cleveland, Grace hailed a taxi to the police station. She had no idea where she would find James, but she knew he would be at the station for his noon meeting with Detective Callahan. Having a few hours to kill, she walked around the city for a while before stopping at a diner for a cup of tea. She was tired. She was worried about James. She wanted to be home with Rosie.

Looking out the window of the little diner, Grace stared off into the distance. Cleveland was a beautiful city beside a lake. Pedestrians strolled through the square, stopping at the fountain in the center of the square. Some sat and ate their lunch; others tossed coins into the fountain and continued on their way. The sky was blue, and the sun was bright. It was a beautiful city. It was hard to envision the ugly sins that the city had to hide.

When the diner clock flashed 11:30, Grace left and headed back towards the police station. Upon entering the station, she stopped at the reception desk and then headed to Detective Callahan's office. Stepping off the elevator, she saw James sitting in a chair outside Callahan's door.

Grace slipped into an alcove, out of his view and took a long hard look at him. She wondered if he was going to be upset with her for showing up. She wondered if she was nothing more than a part of a guilt trip.

"Was he guilty, and am I a way he was trying to alleviate his guilt?" she wondered. The more she dwelt on that thought, the more upset she became.

James had never given her any reason to doubt him. She loved him. Though he never said it, she thought he loved her. At least he gave her a passionate kiss: that had to count for something.

Drying her eyes, Grace stepped out into the hallway and walked towards James. Sitting with his head down and wringing his hat in his hands, James looked up to see Grace standing in front of him. Extending her arms out for a hug, "I'm here for you Babe. I will support you and I believe in you." With tears rolling down her face, "I love you. Please James, let me in."

Chapter 22

"From the Long Arm of the Law"

James was shocked when Grace approached. Never did he expect her to show up in Cleveland, and in some ways he wished she hadn't. He's been down this road of interrogation a time or two. He knew exactly what Detective Callahan would surmise. And he was right.

"Grace." he said. "I know you want answers, and I wish I give you what you need, but right now is not a good time."

Before he could warn her, Detective Callahan appeared from nowhere. "Well, well, well." He said sarcastically: "If it isn't the two love birds? Grace, I was banking you would be here. I could hear it in your voice last evening. How quaint, don't you think?"

The Detective played right into James hands. "You leave her out of this. She has nothing to do with what happened or knows anything about that night!"

"Well, we will see about that, now won't we?" Detective Callahan blurted. "Grace, I am going to have Detective Martin escort you to another room. If that's okay with you!

"I wish you stayed home Grace. They will try to trip your words. Don't let them!" James pleaded.

"How sweet! Trying to be the hero again, now aren't you?" Detective Callahan snorted. "Well, we will see." Looking at his partner, Detective Callahan instructed Grace to be guided to an undesignated area. He then looked at James, waved his hand toward the passageway down the hall, and said: "Shall we? It appears you know the routine."

There, they walked down the long corridor. James traveled to a time he wished he could forget. It was when he felt the country he defended betrayed him. He could feel his blood pressure begin to rise. "Remain calm," he reminded himself.

They finally reached the interrogation room. And James was not disappointed. He was strategically positioned where the bright lights blinded him. "Ok James, you know the routine. I am going to leave you here to gather your thoughts. Would you like something to drink?"

If looks could kill, the police department would be planning a service for the Detective "That's right, James. Go ahead! Stare at me all you want. That's not going to get you out of this mess. I'll be right back sooner or later..." Callahan laughed.

Callahan left James in Interrogation Room 1. Martin showed Grace to an observation room where she could watch the interview. Callahan was soon to join them. He opened the door and stood next to Grace.

"So Grace, how well do you know your new boyfriend?" Callahan asked.

"He and I, well, he's not my boyfriend. James and I have become close over the past year. He has become a big part of my life. We are not in a relationship, but I am in love with him."

Callahan then asked: "Don't you think it is a little strange that you and James moved a little too quickly in a relationship? He stood a lot to gain from your husband's death, don't you think?"

"Many of Ray's friends were a huge support following his death." Grace went on to explain. "I did think it was strange that I had never heard him speak of James, but he knew Ray's greeting and he knew where Ray and I lived. James never gave me any reason to be suspicious. I admit I'm a little suspicious now."

For the record, Grace went on to add: "And I beg to differ Detective, we did not move into a relationship quickly. As I just stated, we are not in a relationship. James has been nothing more than a friend. It wasn't until last night that I told him how I felt."

"Oh come on. Do I look that stupid?" Callahan said without hesitation. "Don't insult my intelligence Mrs. Howard. You stood to gain over $250,000 in life insurance as well as survivor's benefits upon your husband's death. From where I am standing that is motive.

"I was not aware of the death benefits until after Ray's death. I had a pile of paperwork that I had to deal with and that is when I found out about the monetary value of his life insurance and the survivor benefits. I did not come here to be questioned. I came on my own. I really don't have to answer any of your questions."

Callahan then dropped two bombs on Grace. "Do you know what James did before his current job with the power company?" Callahan could tell that Grace was oblivious of James previous occupation. "That's what I thought. He was a trained mercenary for the government. Yes, he has killed before. What makes me think he had nothing to do with your husband's death?" Callahan went on to add: "How do I know you didn't have something to do with it either?"

That was bomb number one. The second bomb followed. "Did you know that James' friend ratted him out?" He could tell he struck a blow to Grace's opinion regarding James.

"Yes, his friend Larry Lancaster informed us that he witnessed an altercation between James and Raymond in the parking lot that fatal night. He felt it was his civic obligation to let us know. He protected James long enough."

Grace's mind raced back to the parking lot where she found the credit card stub bearing the name Larry. Grace was in fact wearing the same jacket she wore that night. It was the last time she wore it. She reached into her pocket and pulled out the receipt. "Isn't it possible someone else knows more about what happened that night? When I visited Cleveland shortly after Ray's death, I found this slip blowing in the parking lot."

Grace handed the detective the credit card receipt. "It's dated the same evening Ray was killed. It is possible that if you find this person, you will have a witness to whatever happened in that parking lot".

"Miss Howard, we will see what you think of James after I am finished." Callahan said confidently. "And based on the outcome, don't be too terribly shocked when you suffer the same fate. What do you have to say about that?

"I think you are wrong. I loved Ray." Grace said with tears rolling down her cheeks. "James may have been in the bar with Ray the night he died, but I find it hard to believe he killed him." Grace went on. "I would know. I would feel it."

Callahan looked at the paper Grace handed him. He raised his eyebrows when he saw the signature at the bottom.

He blew it off as mere coincidence. But even his instincts started to scream "foul ball!"

He chuckled. "We will see! Martin, make sure you do a background check on Larry. Let's make sure we cover our bases before we close the books on this one. Callahan left the observation room and walked back into Interrogation Room 1.

Callahan did not beat around the bush. "So James, did you ever murder anyone?" he asked.

"No! Not to my recollection." James responded.

James did not see it coming. Callahan tossed his service jacket on the table. "Let me rephrase the question. Have you ever killed anyone?"

Callahan hit a nerve with James. His service record was sealed. He sat silent.

"Oh! You are pleading the fifth, I see. It seems to me that you have dodged the long arm of the law for some time." Callahan said. "Does November 26, 1984 ring a bell or two? What about the name Markland?"

James clearly understood that Grace was witnessing this interrogation. She asked him to let her in his life. Unfortunately it was under such circumstances. He looked at the glass and answered the question. "Yes, sir, I remember that date all too well." James replied. "I wish it never happened, sir. But I was following orders."

"Tell me soldier." Callahan asked. "Where is it in the Military Code of Justice that states you practically decapitate a fellow soldier?"

Angered, James shot back: "It is something you would never understand. It is something you could never understand."

"Really?" Believing he had James on the ropes, Callahan went so far as to open an old wound. "Even your government betrayed you. How does that make you feel?" He asked: "Explain it to me then. No, better yet, explain it to Grace. You know she is watching this line of questioning. Does she know you have this insatiable appetite to kill?"

"You leave her out of this! She had nothing to do with that evening." James had just opened the door.

"So you do know something about her husband's death!" Callahan felt like he just threw the game winning pitch.

"No, sir, I don't." James swung. "All I remember is that her husband and I said some words in the parking lot. The rest is a blur."

Leaning up against the window, softly crying, Grace placed her hand on the window "No James, no," she said.

"That's funny you should say that." Callahan added. "Your friend Larry tells us differently. He said you had everything to do with Raymond's death."

Hearing those words, everything started to make sense. That's why Larry called James the following morning. He wanted to see how much James remembered. Larry was fully aware of James' past. He was there when James blacked out. "James didn't do it." Grace said to herself.

"It was Larry!" James shouted. "Larry is the one who threw the fatal blow. It all makes sense now!"

"Nice try soldier. Go ahead and blame your friend." Callahan shot back.

"No! No!" James pleaded. "Believe me, it was Larry. He followed me out to the parking lot. He was infuriated with Raymond for not standing up like a man. Raymond tried to ignore his nonsense. Larry had nothing of it." James added.

"Detective Martin, Larry was in the parking lot that night! I think he could have set James up to take the fall." Grace pleaded.

James went on to explain. "I blanked out when he said the words: 'Te amo.' It reminded me of that night on November 26, 1984. When I woke up, Raymond had already transpired. I panicked. I ran back home."

Detective Martin opened the door. "Sir, we need to talk." There was a sense of urgency in Martin's voice.

"Can't it wait?" Callahan inquired.

"No, sir, it can't!" Martin said.

Callahan left James to reflect on the conversation they just had. "What is it, Martin?" Callahan demanded to know.

"Sir, I just did a background check on Larry. He has a history of violence." Martin informed his partner. "I tried calling his place of employment. His boss informed me that Larry did not show up for work this morning."

"Get to your point, Martin." Callahan wanted to know.

"Well, sir." Martin added. "Surveillance on the Turnpike has caught Larry leaving the state. I believe Larry is the one who is running from the long arm of the law."

Chapter 23

"Free as a Bird"

GRACE TURNED HER HEAD TOWARD Detectives Martin and Callahan. She had a puzzled look on her face, "A year later, Larry comes forward to point the finger at James, and then he flees? It doesn't make sense." Grace stated. Her head was spinning. "Am I free to go?"

When Detective Martin motioned towards the door, Grace fled. She had no idea where she was going, but she knew she did not want to see James just yet. The man she was in love with hidden the fact that he was there and a part of the altercation in the parking lot.

Dizzy, confused, and nauseated, she looked up towards the heavens as if expecting an answer. Seeing the bell tower of a nearby church, she made her way through traffic and entered. Seeking solace, solitude, and not wanting to face James, she found sanctuary in the church.

Grace spent the afternoon comforted by the cross in front of the church. She carried on a one-way conversation with Ray. She prayed to her Heavenly Father for a decision that would bring her peace.

Unaware of how much time had passed, Grace was surprised that it was dusk when she emerged from the church. "I need to find a car." She said realizing she needed to head back to New York. Panic started to set in. She didn't have her purse or her overnight bag.

"The Police Station! I left my things at the Police Station." Grace headed back to retrieve her belongings. As she entered the lobby, she saw James sitting there.

"My gosh, Grace, where have you been? I've been worried sick about you." James said.

"You've been here all this time?" she asked.

"I saw your airline ticket in your bag. I knew you didn't have a way back to New York."

Grace was not prepared to see James and wasn't sure how to respond. On one hand, she despised him for hiding his involvement with Ray. On the other hand, she loved him. Grace knew first hand that soldiers were often haunted by their past. Grace had lost friends to suicide; soldiers that could not cope with things they had to do while in battle. Grace had witnessed her own father go through breakdowns. She had heard Ray talk of his men and the trials and tribulations they went through when returning from the fields of battle. Grace knew that some soldiers were ticking time bombs and little things would set them off.

Something transpired that night in the parking lot. It was no fault of Rays, nor was it any fault of James. One might chalk it up to bad timing, a misfortunate accident. James was penitent. He wronged a brother, but then done right by him. Grace and Rosie were his act of contrition. James could have walked away after the altercation in the parking lot. But he didn't. Instead, he gave up everything he had ever known. He moved to New York to ensure that Ray's wife and daughter would be all right.

Grace had spent many hours in the cathedral that afternoon wrestling with all sorts of demons. She came to Cleveland to support James. That is where she wanted to be. She desired to be next to him. It would be a hurdle to be dealt with; that's what prayer and counseling are for.

"Please let me take you home," James said as he handed Grace her belongings. Grace nodded in affirmation and together they walked to the parking garage. James put her bag in the trunk and then opened the car door for her. It would be a long seven-hour drive to New York.

Grace said not a word. She sat gazing out the passenger window. "Grace, will you talk to me? What's on your mind? Please say something." The silence was killing James. Grace reached her hand over and laid it on his leg. James locked his hand in hers. Grace closed her eyes and fell asleep.

Chapter 24

"RING AROUND A ROSIE"

I T WAS EARLY MORNING WHEN James and Grace drove up to her parent's house. They were exhausted. Outside of kissing Rosie goodnight, the only thing on their minds was sleep. What they weren't expecting was to see the gravel road lined and littered with squad cars. The flashing lights from squad cars disturbed the sullenness and stillness of the early morning darkness.

They could barely make out the silhouettes of officers as they stood against their vehicles with their weapons drawn. They could faintly hear an officer speaking through his bullhorn. Just as the officers' weapons were drawn to the house, so too were the words of the officer. "Come out with your hands up" were the only words they could make out.

A barricade forced James to stop the car. "What in the world is going on?" he questioned. "When will they leave us alone?" he said agitated. He had no choice but to park on the side of the road. He looked over at Grace. He was beyond words. All he could mutter was: "It's hard for me to say I'm sorry."

Grace shook her head in disbelief. She and James exited the car and started their walk towards the squadron of vehicles. They were immediately stopped when one of the officers commanded that they not advance any further.

Taking the initiative, James abruptly asked: "What's going on officer? If it is me you are after, I promise to turn myself over to the authorities without incident."

"Sir, I wish it were that easy," the officer replied. "Do you live here?"

"No, this is my parent's home." Grace said with a trembling voice.

"I am sorry, ma'am. We have a hostage crisis." The officer said as a matter of fact. "The occupants of the home are being held against their will, ma'am. We are doing the best we can to negotiate with the perpetrator."

James lunged toward the house only to be met by a swarm of officers. "That's far enough Superman!" The team leader shouted. "We need for you and the Misses to please stand down and to the side. Let us do our jobs!"

"Oh dear God, Rosie!" Grace whispered.

"Are you her mother, ma'am?" The officer asked sympathetically.

Grace could barely speak. She was numb. She was in a state of shock. She was not equipped to handle everything that happened: the trip to Cleveland earlier, the interrogation, the long ride home, and now this. It was all too much. She could barely speak. "Yes." She faintly responded, followed by fainting.

James caught her before she fully collapsed to the ground. He carried off to the side lawn where he gently laid her on the soft grass. As he did a year prior at the Marriott, he held her head in the palms of his hands.

The officer noticed two sides to James. He was witnessing the caring and compassionate side. But as James continued to reflect upon the crisis before them, the officer noticed a combatant side. He could see it in James' eyes. They were cold; they were blank; and they were lifeless. Whoever was holding Grace's family hostage pulled a trigger in James.

"Now, sir!" The officer tried to explain. "Before you decide to become a superhero, don't do anything stupid."

"No one!" James thought. "And I mean no one will ever harm one hair of my family. Not on my watch."

James countered with the command: "Yes, sir!" He then proceeded to care for Grace, as her body lay limp. After some time, she came too. She looked up to James and while sobbing asked: "What are we going to do?"

Chapter 25

"Just Walk Away"

J AMES AND GRACE SAT QUIETLY until they heard the culprit's voice scream out to the officers. "Larry!" James said under his breath.

He turned to Grace. "It is Larry!" He harshly whispered. He realized how his tone greatly affected Grace. Every time Larry blurted something out from the window, James' anger intensified. And every time his anger intensified, Grace's anxiety increased in direct proportion.

Grace struggled to wrap her mind between what had happened and what was happening. She could not stand the thought of losing her parents, but more importantly, Rosie. She already lost Raymond because of Larry, now this. "How much more must I suffer at the hands of this madman?" she thought.

She started to tremble again. Grace was going into shock. Sensing her distress, James put his arm around her and promised her that no harm was going to come to her family.

"That's easy for you to say," she cried. "It's not your family in there." Though James was well aware of the obvious, they weren't his family, Grace's words served as knife piercing the aorta. They cut to his heart.

"Grace is right." James reminded himself. "They are not his family. This has nothing to do with him, but it had everything to do with them."

"Come on Grace, let's go!" He said.

"Where?" She asked.

"I am going to take you to a squad car. You are shivering and you need to stay warm." Grace mistook his calm demeanor as a strike against him. It served as a point taken to the point she just drove home a few moments ago. "It was not his family."

Angry with James for his lack of emotion, Grace snapped and barked out: "Don't you care? Why do you always have to be so strong?"

If she only knew how much James did care for her and her family. Sadly, though, the human eye can only see what appears on the outside and, at times, is blind to the inner workings of something within someone.

What Grace did not see was how James' emotions allowed him to experience a feeling he had not had in such a very long time. It was the fear factor. James, for the first time in a long time, was afraid. He was afraid of losing Grace, of Grace losing her family, and of never being fully forgiven for his past and now his present. He was afraid of being alone. Like Grace, James too was overwhelmed.

Realizing his presence around Grace was doing more harm than good, he got her situated in the back of a squad car and then politely excused himself

"Where are you going?" Grace demanded to know. "You can't just leave me sitting here by myself!"

Withholding his tears, James turned away and walked away. Grace could see how his figure became one with the darkness. He was gone. James had disappeared.

"That's right, James!" Grace yelled. "Just do what you do best: "WALK AWAY!"

Chapter 26

"GRACE PRAYS FOR GRACE: A MOTHER'S PLEA"

I N THE REFUGE OF A police cruiser, Grace closed her eyes and leaned her head against the window. Tired from the long drive and exhausted from the interrogation by the Cleveland detectives, her head was pounding. Her baby was trapped along with her parents. They were now held captive by a crazed man who had just a year ago, murdered her husband. "And James, James just walked away."

"How did things turn so crazy," she wondered. On the drive home from Cleveland, she felt an unspoken bond between her and James. She felt at peace. She felt comfort. "Why did he just walk away?" Grace replayed in her mind over and over the hurtful words she said to him: "It's not your family in there." But it was his family in there.

Rosie was two when Ray died. She didn't remember him. James was the only man that resembled a father. Rosie adored him. She often called James, "Daddy". Grace didn't bother to correct her. When Rosie said her prayers at night, she always thanked God for sending her James.

One of the ladies at church Sunday school told Rosie, "God answers prayers." Rosie prayed for a daddy, and James showed up. James was not just the answer to Rosie's prayers, but Graces as well.

Sitting in the back of the cruiser, Grace prayed for the safety of her family. She prayed for the wisdom on how to fix things between her and James. She needed him to know that her family was his family. Grace wanted nothing more than to be his wife.

"Please, please, please, let them be alright," she said with a shiver running down her spine.

Chapter 27

"WHERE'S JAMES?"

SOME TIME HAD ELAPSED SINCE James quietly excused himself from the scene. Grace was still sitting in the back of the squad car as negotiations with Larry stalled. Larry had one request and one request only: "He wanted to personally speak with James."

The lead negotiator eventually succumbed to Larry's demands. He went to the squad car furthest from the scene. There he found Grace. She was sitting alone. "Where's James?" he asked.

Grace shook her head, "I don't know." She said bitterly. "He just up and walked away."

"How long ago was that?" he asked.

Grace looking down really could not answer his question. She was still angry, agitated, and alone. "Maybe an hour or so," She estimated.

"Ma'am, which direction did he head?" The negotiator asked. "He has been summoned by Larry. We really do need to find him."

Grace with her head still down, pointed in the direction where James' disappeared into the darkness. Without ever realizing it, James had walked toward a back trail to the house. Most people were not fully aware of its existence since the woods covered it. Those who lived on the property used it.

The officer asked Grace if she knew where her finger pointing led. Grace had no choice but to follow her finger. Instantly, she knew where James went. He was going to settle a score. Her instincts told her what he was up to, but her instructions to the officers ran contrary.

"I don't know!" Grace said. "I believe it leads to some woods that eventually dead-end at the interstate."

The officer walked away discouraged. "Ma'am, thank you. We will see what we can do to resolve this issue as soon as possible."

"Oh, James! I hope you know what you are doing?" She murmured and then prayed. "I don't know why, but I trust you! Please bring my baby back to me."

She could hear the negotiator speak over the bullhorn. "I'm sorry, sir. James is not in a position to speak with you."

"What are you talking about?" Larry said nervously. "I want to talk with him now!"

Shots fired from inside the house exacerbated Grace's emotions. Moments later she saw her father emerge from the wooded path with Rosie in his arms and her mother beside him. Running up to them, "How did you manage to get out of the house?

"James." Her father said. "He snuck in the house while Larry was talking with the police. Never did he notice that James snuck in through the basement door.

Puzzled by the shots fired, Grace had to know. "Who or what was Larry shooting?"

"Nothing, I think." Grace's father said. "We believe it was a nervous reaction. When the police told him that Jim was not in a position to speak, Larry went ballistic, so to speak."

"Is James in there right now?" Grace wanted to know. She had to know.

"I believe he is honey. I have a strange feeling there is some unfinished business that James needs to address."

Giving his daughter a hug, "Grace, James requested I share two thoughts with you." Her father went on to say. "The first thing did not make any sense, but he wanted you to know that 'It was hard for him to say he was sorry.'" Her father could tell that Grace fully comprehended James' concern.

The second thing was just a potent and as powerful as the first. "He also wanted me to let you know that 'yes, he does love you very much." Grace's heart melted. Her lip quivered and she cried with joy. Those tearful sobs of joy, however, were quickly exchanged for anger. "Why could he not have said something earlier? He always has to have the last word."

Chapter 28

"BE CAREFUL WHAT YOU WISH FOR."

LARRY PRACTICALLY WENT THROUGH THE roof when he heard James voice behind him. "Here I am Larry," James said. "What is it that you want to say to me?"

Of all people, it was Larry who understood James like the back of his hand. They grew up together. They shared everything together: well, almost everything. Larry had become so consumed with the officers outside; he failed to secure the entire house. Not that would have made any difference.

James was a trained professional. It's like riding a bike, as some say. Once you learn, you never forget. James would have gained entry one way or another. There really was not much Larry could have done to escape this final bout between what was once a great friendship.

It was not long that Larry realized he lost his bargaining chips. He was at the poker table empty-handed: well, almost empty-handed. Though James freed Grace's parents and Rosie while Larry talked with the negotiators, Larry did still have his gun.

Before James accepted Larry's invitation to talk, he instructed Grace's family to follow the same path James did. There, they would find Grace. Cracking his knuckles as if to rumble, James asked Larry a second time: "What compelled you to take this family hostage and want to talk to me?"

Larry nervously laughed. "Come on, James. We have been friends since we were little kids, man. Doesn't that mean anything? Doesn't that count for something?"

"A person with half a brain would think?" James shot back. "Tell me, Larry. Why? Why kill an innocent man?"

"He wasn't as innocent as you think?" Larry snarled. "It was because of him that I was discharged under circumstances other than honorable."

James stood silent. He let Larry finish. "That's right, man! He ruined my career in the military! You didn't know that, did you?"

Somber, James answered: "No." But James knew Larry to be ill tempered. "What was it you did, Larry?"

"Nothing deserving of what I received." Larry continued. "Some stupid kid fresh from training got smart with me one night. He was green as the grass outside. He was fine as the sand that blew around that forsaken and foreign land we were called to defend."

"Somebody had to teach the snot nose recruit a lesson." Larry went on to justify his actions.

"Let me guess," James chided. "You were that somebody, right Larry?"

"You are dang right! I beat that boy to a pulp." Larry said, congratulating himself. "When I was finished with him, he didn't have to worry about fighting in that God forsaken war anymore! I sent that boy packing for the States," Larry said. "I did that boy a favor!"

"Really?" James inquired. "How?"

"He's alive today isn't he? He may have died in battle!"

"That's true!" James said firmly. "Larry how is he today?"

"Bound to a wheelchair, he is! But at least he's alive." Larry grumbled. "And besides, don't you judge me. At least I didn't slit his throat."

James clearly remembered how the "bullet ants" stung him the night in question. He could recall every sensation that ran through his central nervous system. But they never hit a nerve like Larry did. Trying to maintain his composure, James asked: "So why did you kill Ray Howard? "

"Because he refused to even look my way that evening in the bar. I recognized him from the moment he sat down. And you can't tell me that he didn't know who I was," Larry argued. "When I saw you go out to confront him, I took my chances." Larry somewhat laughed.

"You should have seen yourself man. As soon as the dude started to speak that Spanish crap, you went blank. I seized the opportunity to punch him in the throat so hard he gasped until his final breath." Larry said bragging. "And you, my friend passed out like a little baby!"

Still trying to remain composed, James asked: "So why set me up? What did I ever do to you?"

"Man, you are dumber than I thought," Larry argued. "You were never supposed to get involved with the dude's wife! You always had to be the 'hero!' You are no different than I am."

James smiled. "You are right Larry!" Look outside. Larry turned for a moment to see Rosie and her grandparents reunited with Grace.

"Dude!" James said confidently. "Let's end this. I let you speak; now it's my turn. Etas mano y mano!"

Larry started to shake. He knew that when it came to military strategy and skill, he was no match for James. There they stood: "mano y mano."

"You got what you asked for," James said sarcastically. "I am here. Go ahead, Larry, make your move."

Chapter 29

"Reunited Feels So Good"

OUTSIDE ON THE LAWN GRACE stood with her parents. She remembered James was a trained mercenary, "Oh my gosh! Please James don't do anything stupid" Grace said under her breath. "Dad, someone has to stop James before he does anything to Larry. I don't want him to go to prison!"

Grace ran toward the house yelling "James, James, NO! Don't do anything stupid." Two officers chased her down and pulled her off the porch before she made it through the front door.

One of the officers dragged Grace away from the house kicking and screaming. "James, DO NOT DO ANYTHING STUPID! DON'T KILL HIM JAMES! I love you! I need you! Walk away James! Walk away!"

In a state of panic thinking that James would kill Larry, Grace flailed, trying to break free of the policeman's hold. Seeing his daughter in such a state, the Command Sergeant Major slipped back down the path and into his house. Yelling out to James, his voice boomed, "Son, son, leave the justice to the police. You have a life with Grace and Rosie. Don't throw your life away over a dishonorable soldier."

Still facing off with Larry, James bellowed, "Thank you, sir! However, we have some unsettled business to attend to."

Larry nervously laughed. In some ways, he wished his ordeal with James was over. His face said it all. He was scared. Rather than breaking the two men apart, Grace's father, having served in the military, honored the soldier's code and retreated from his own home.

James then asked for permission to "Carry-On!" There was a part of Larry hoping that Graces' dad denied the request, but he didn't. "Permission granted. Carry on soldier!"

The Command Sergeant Major understood very well the desire for revenge. He knew James would make the right decision for himself.

Grace heaved a sigh of relief when she saw her father walking towards where she along with her mother and Rosie were sitting on the lawn. Rosie sat in her mother's lap, oblivious to the seriousness of what had just happened.

Grace, tired and haggard sat quietly taking it all in. Waves of guilt swept through her. "I should not have gone off to Cleveland chasing after James." She thought to herself. She hugged Rosie harder. Her mother did not deserve what Larry had subjected her family too. Grace studied the lines on her mother's face.

Grace got to her feet and wrapped her arms around her dad and cried: "I'm sorry Dad. This is my entire fault." To Grace, the booming Command Sergeant Major has been just Dad. Grace's parents were aging. Today brought out their vulnerability. Grace could no longer see her dad as the vibrant solider and protector of the country. He was an old man that could have easily died this day right along with her mother and daughter.

Grace's mother put her arm around her daughter and said: "Everything will work out. It always does dear. Have faith."

As they stood with their arms wrapped around one another, Grace's father led a prayer of thanks to God for the safety of family, which included James. They waited with great anticipation to see James emerge from the family home.

After the "Amen," Grace had to know. "How is James?"

Her father smiled: "He's fine, my dear. He's not the one you need to be concerned with."

"Why didn't you talk him down Dad?"

"Sweetie, I have been in the military for many years. I have seen just about everything a person could ever see."

Grace interrupted her father's little speech. "How could you just leave him in there? Did you see anything?"

"Please let me finish Grace." Her father politely said. He always had a soothing way of calming her. "I saw a man who had a score to settle. I saw a soldier ready to defend the people he loves even it meant death. I have this gut feeling, James will do what's right. He will work it out."

Grace's father then laughed to himself. "I sure do feel sorry for his friend though."

Chapter 30

"Do Not Repay Evil for Evil"

AND SO THERE THE TWO men stood. They were pitted against one another. Friends since childhood were now foes. James did not flinch. He sized up his opponent. Every sense in his body went on high alert.

"Well, Larry?" James asked. "Aren't you going to do something? I am waiting for you to make the first move. At least then, my mind might have reason to call it a justifiable homicide."

Once again, Larry started to laugh nervously. "I don't know about you James, but it seems I have a firm grip on things. I am holding a 9 mm semi-automatic pistol. There is no more than twenty feet separating us. I don't care how well trained you are: you can't stop a bullet now can you?"

"A person would almost think so," James said calmly. "So, what is stopping you from pulling the trigger? Or are you the coward I believe you to be?"

"James, my old time friend, I do not believe you are in a position to make any snide remarks," Larry chided. "The odds are stacked against you."

"A person would almost think so?" James said remaining composed. "If you are so confident, then make your move. You are a coward!"

"Who are you calling a coward? You fool! I am going to take you out!" Larry sounded.

"I am looking forward to it!" James shouted. "Come on man: do it! You know as well as I do, it's over! Just pull the dang trigger. You will be doing me and the world a favor."

"What about your little girlfriend and her daughter?" Larry tried using them as a bargaining chip. "I thought you two were an item."

James was losing his patience. He was not in the mood for playing any more games. "Since when did you start caring for others?" He shot back. "As I see it, you have two choices: do something or surrender. "Either way, you are going down."

Larry started to lose it. He feared James. "That's true my old friend. I more than likely will go down. But I am not going without a fight. I am taking you with me."

With that, Larry raised his pistol to take aim at James. He shuddered when he saw James smiling. "You think this is funny?" Larry said anxiously.

"No, Larry. I don't," James regretfully said. "I find it extremely sad. And by the way, Larry, thank you!"

"What should I be thanking you for?" Larry asked in a state of confusion.

"By taking aim, you have just given me permission to do what I am about to do." James answered.

"What might…?" Larry started to say. But James was not going to give him the privilege to finish his question. James thought it was best to end this ordeal. Instead of saying it, James rather would have Larry see it.

Before Larry could move a muscle or his mind, he was on the floor. He was holding his left thigh. The pain was beyond belief. Larry couldn't believe it as well. He never saw it coming. It was that quick. James in one continuous motion reached down to his right ankle, grabbed the knife from underneath his pant leg, and flung it at Larry.

Larry had no time to react to James' reflexes. James walked toward his opponent, pulled the knife from Larry's thigh, raised Larry's head and put the blade against his throat. Crying, Larry blurted out: "So you are going to kill me like you did your friend! I guess it doesn't pay to be a friend of yours.

Those words set of a host of emotions in James. His mind went traveling through time. He remembered how Markland pleaded for James to end his life. For a second, Larry gained an upper hand. Larry could tell that he diverted James' attention. But that distraction was brief. It was broken up when James heard Grace's screams outside.

He snapped out of his state of mind just as quickly as he slipped into it. "It's not going to work this time!" James said. "It's over and you, my friend, are done. I am finishing what you started!" James started to press the knife tightly to Larry's neck. He was about to swipe the edge of the blade across Larry's throat when he heard a voice from the past.

Ironically, Larry heard it as well. As the voice started to speak, the room produced a glow that was visible to everyone outside. "Don't James! That's not how you want to end this," the voice firmly said.

"Markland!" James cried aloud. "Is that you?"

"You have fought the battle that needed to be fought. You have always wanted to know the answer to the question 'Why?' Now you know, my dear friend. Let justice take care of itself. As the Good Book says: 'Do not repay evil for evil (Romans 12:4: NKJV)."

James cried like he never cried before. "Markland! It's so hard for me to say I am sorry!"

"You don't need to feel guilty anymore. That night you spared me from suffering more than I had too. I must be going my friend.'

Upon those words, the room returned to its natural luminescence. James, still pressing his weapon tightly against Larry's neck, whispered into Larry's ear. "I guess it's your lucky day." He then hit Larry squarely in the back of the head knocking him out.

Chapter 31

"WHERE'S JAMES?"

P OLICE SWARMED THE INSIDE OF the house; only to
find Larry lying on the floor unconscious. He was in
need of some medical attention subsequent to the stab
wound in his thigh. James' knife was found stuck in the floor
with a note. It had some scribbling on it.

It read: "To Grace. It's hard for me to say I am sorry."

They searched every inch of the house, but James was
gone. He exited the residence as he entered it. He slipped out
of the home like water through the fingers.

Chaos now filled the home as reporters were catching
up on the scoop and police were searching and processing
evidence.

James' walked along the darkened trail. From a distance,
he could still see the flashing lights as they pierced through
the darkness. Eventually, James would be enveloped by
darkness. He was not sure where he was going or what he
was going to do.

He honestly believed he found happiness with Grace and
in Grace. His thoughts took him in every possible direction.
He could not digest the possibility of living life without her.

108

His biggest regret was he never sharing how he truly felt. But then, he was trained not to feel; not to show any emotion. But emotion was all he had. He wanted to share it with her.

Making his way to the interstate, James walked on the inside of the guardrail. He did not want to be spotted by oncoming traffic, but more importantly, by those who may be searching for him. At that point in time, he needed to reflect, to meditate, and to pray.

In the distance, he believed he heard a rushing river at the base of the ravine. He followed the sound of its flow. Grabbing onto one tree to the next, James used his hands to guide him down the steep path. His instincts were dead on. It was a river.

Over the years, for some strange reason, the sound of water always spoke to James. It brought peace to his soul. Maybe it was the river's rhythm of rushing water or maybe it was water's power to cleanse, he wasn't sure, but it was his sanctuary.

He sat down along the river's bank deep in thought. He leaned against a tree. He looked into the stars for some sign or sort of direction to set his sails on. Desperation started to consume him. He wanted so desperately to be with Grace and Rosie. But what reason did have to return to them? Grace made it pretty clear that he was not considered part of her family.

To belong! That's all he wished for. That's all he wanted. How he longed to be part of something bigger and better. How his heart yearned to be part of a family and to have a family he could call his own.

He drifted back to the night in Honduras. He envied Markland. At least Markland was at peace. At least Markland was now made perfect.

James could not help but think about how a part of him died that evening. He picked up a small smooth stone and threw it in the river. Where it landed, he could not tell. All he could do was hear it splash as it broke the surface of the water.

He closed his eyes and dozed off. He dreamt about the stone he just threw. He dreamt that he was that stone. It splashed into the fast moving current only to be swept downstream. Its destination had yet to be determined. But in the process, that stone would toss and turn with each new stroke of each new current. Eventually, it would come to the end of its course. Its final resting place would be found in the fine silt of some riverbed. That stone, once it became lodged from the pressures above and the place below, would drown; it would surrender and succumb to its environment: probably never to be seen again.

While dreaming, James' heart raced. He started to feel suffocated. He could feel the pressures of the water bearing down on his chest. He tried to fight his way to the surface; the river was too swift and too strong. He cried out for help, there was none to be found. He was alone. He was by himself.

He found the strength to poke his head above the water one last time. He drew his last breath before being completely swallowed. He was able to catch a glimpse to the river's shore. There he saw Grace. She was reaching out with her arms begging him to take hold. She was there to help.

James tried to reach out to her. Just then his dream was disturbed as some angry ants made their way up his leg and stung him. James jumped to his feet. "Dang ants!" He shouted. Though he brushed them off as best he could; he had more important things to attend to.

The sun was breaking over the horizon. It was a new day. It was a new dawn. And James was not going to drown by the current. He was going to grab the hand of the one who could help him. He started to double-time it to Grace's.

Chapter 32

"MOMMY, IS JAMES COMING BACK?"

WITH JAMES NOWHERE TO BE found, Rosie, Grace and her parents headed to Grace's house where they shared stories about the happenings of the day before. Grace put on a pot of coffee and made breakfast for her parents. Rosie fell asleep on the coach.

"Honey, what are you going to do about James?" Her mother asked.

"I don't know Mom. I just don't know." Grace said with a saddened heart.

It was just a little past noon when Grace's parents left. They headed to the military police department to file a formal statement. Grace picked a sleeping Rosie up from the sofa and tucked her into bed. She crawled in next to her, but sleep would not come so easily for Grace. She buried her face into the soft curls on Rosie's head and wept.

Rosie's stirring woke Grace up. It was a little past six. Rosie snuggled up against her mother. Grace lay there staring at the ceiling. She wished she could have taken back the hurtful words she said to James that morning. "He is part of this family." Grace thought to herself. "It took a long time for him to open up and I think I blew it."

A squeaky little voice brought Grace back to reality. "I love you Mommy."

Grace wrapped her arms around Rosie, "I love you too sweetie."

"Is James coming home, Mommy?" Rosie asked so innocently.

"No Sweetie. I don't think we will be seeing James this evening."

"Can I call him Mommy? I have something important to tell him."

"What do you want to tell James, Sweetie?"

"Mommy, I want to tell him I love him."

"I think James would like to hear that."

"How about we get cleaned up and change our clothes. We'll call James and see if he'll meet us for pie at Pie Guy's?" Rosie gave her mom a hug and headed towards the bathtub. Grace ran a comb through her hair and put clean clothes on. Now out of the tub, Rosie bounded down the steps dancing eagerly around the telephone.

"I'm sorry Rosie." Grace said. "He's not answering his phone."

Disappointment crossed Rosie's little face. "You and I can still go." She said to Rosie.

"It won't be the same Mommy." Grabbing her jacket, Rosie stepped out on the porch to wait for her mother.

"Mommy, Mommy, he's here!" Seeing James on the porch swing, Rosie crawled up into his lap. She wrapped her little arms around his neck and gave him a sloppy wet kiss. "I love you James!"

Grace's heart skipped a beat when she saw them together. Feeling light headed and her knees going weak, "James," was all Grace managed to get out before the tears started rolling. "How long have you been sitting out here?" Grace sat next to James on the swing.

Visibly shaken, Grace felt every emotion good and bad running through her mind. Shock could not describe how she felt seeing James on the porch. Not sure what to say or do, she sat there a little dumbfounded.

Rosie on the other hand was elated to see James. She excitedly told him that they were going for pie. It was something that Rosie and her mom often did on the weekend. Rosie missed James and wanted him to join in on the special treat.

For Grace, inviting James to accompany them to the local pie shop seemed like such a diminutive step after all they had been through, but to Rosie, it was a significant event.

"Come with us Daddy. Please, come with us, please!" Rosie pleaded.

James hoisted Rosie up onto his shoulders, "I'd love to sweetie." With Rosie on his shoulders, James wrapped his hands around her calves making sure she was secure on her perch. Grace wriggled her finger through one of James' belt loops as they headed down the sidewalk together.

"See Mommy, we are a real family!" Rosie said as a matter of fact.

Grace felt the electricity in the air. Sparks were flying between her and James.

Chapter 33

"Marry Me"

Rosie did much of the talking in the little café. Unaware of the dangerous situation she was thrust in the middle of the early morning, the only thing Rosie picked up on was the excitement of the day. Grace and James ate their pie in silence, stealing glances at one another. Rosie's little body was exhausted and running on adrenaline. Grace was happy for that, with Rosie jabbering away, it saved her from having to make small talk with James.

The last meaningful thing Grace told James was "I love you." And then hell fire and brimstone fell from the sky. Before getting up from the table, Grace took hold of James' hand, "I'm sorry James. I know we are your family. I know that. My parents think the world of you."

James carried Rosie as he and Grace headed back towards the house. He took Rosie's sleeping body upstairs and tucked her into bed. He then knelt beside her bed, took her hand in his, and said a prayer over her.

Grace was waiting for James at the foot of the stairs. Taking him by the hand, she fell into the sofa and pulled James down on top of her. Running her hands under the back of his shirt, she pulled it over his head. Grace ran her hands up his back and over his shoulders tracing the definition of his chiseled muscles.

Neither spoke a word. Pushing her hair off to the side, James buried his face into Grace's neck. His hot breath sent chills down her spine. The last thing Grace heard before drifting off to sleep was: "Marry me Grace Howard."

Chapter 34

"THE TEA PARTY"

THE SOUND OF SQUEALS AND laughter woke Grace. She was surprised to find herself tucked comfortably in her own bed. A breeze blew the bedroom curtains. Rays of sunshine danced into the room. Slipping out of bed, she padded down the hall and peeked in on Rosie. The small table in her room was set for a tea party. Rosie rocked a teddy bear in her lap. Grace could see that Rosie was reading a book to the bear.

The aroma of fresh coffee turned Grace's attention to the downstairs. Grace brushed her teeth and freshened up and then headed downstairs. Passing through the living room, she could see that James spent the night on the sofa.

James was at the stove. Grace came up behind him and wrapped her arms around his waist. "Go away Grace, you are going to ruin the surprise."

"What are you talking about James?" James turned from the stove and looked down at Grace. He pulled her close and held her tight. She could feel his body tremble: he was crying. She tried to pull away, but he tightened his hold.

"Go wait in Rosie's room. I'll be up in a minute."

"Good morning Rosie Sunshine, what a beautiful table you set for Mr. Bear."

"Good morning Mommy," Rosie said, giving her mother a big hug. "It's a surprise tea party. Sit down here Mommy." Rosie said, pointing to a little chair at the table.

Grace and Rose were seated at the little table in Rosie's bedroom when James walked in carrying a tray full of pancakes, eggs, bacon, coffee, juice, and tea. Looking at Rosie James asked: "Do you have it?" Rosie nodded her head 'yes' and patted her little teapot.

James placed the breakfast tray on top of Rosie's dresser. Taking Grace's left hand, he dropped to one knee and said, "Grace Howard, would you do me the honor of being my wife?" And then he nodded to Rosie. Rosie grabbed her little teapot spilling its contents onto the table.

Grace sat speechless as James picked up an antique amethyst ring and slid it on her finger. "Grace, there has been nothing typical about our relationship. A diamond would not do justice to our unique bond. The amethyst is said to strengthen relationships and give its wearer courage. Please say 'yes.'"

Chapter 35

"The Mission"

Grace and James exchanged their vows on a picturesque autumn day. The colors that lined the sky as the trees announced a new seasoned came to symbolize Grace and James past and now their present. The leaves gently blew in the breeze, reminding everyone that just as there is seasons in nature, so too, are there seasons of the soul.

Their guests were moved as the newly found and formed couple expressed their undying devotion and love for one another. They had been through so much in such a short time, yet through it all, their commitment was strengthened and the conjugal bonds they now shared were sealed.

Grace's parents had the honor of watching their daughter begin a new life. They kept Rosie as James and Grace consummated their marriage by traveling to a remote village hidden in the hills of Honduras. Though James did not explain the purpose for wanting to spend his honeymoon in such a small part of the world, Grace never asked.

Upon entering this small dot on the map, many villagers greeted James. If Grace were not mistaken, she would have thought James knew them and they knew James. And her suspicions were correct. James owed his life to them.

One of the ladies who cared for James some years ago, slowly walked up to him, only to put her arms around him. She asked him: "Todavia me recuerdas?"

James extended his arm. Holding her by the shoulders, he looked his friend in the face and responded: "Como podria olvidarte?" Feeling like a square peg in a round hole, Grace started to show signs of uneasiness. Like typical Grace, she had to know what they were saying.

"James!" she demanded. "What did you two say to one another? And how do you know them."

James smiled. Of the many things he loved about Grace, her insistence and persistence were ranked at the top of his list. ""She asked me if had forgotten about her?' and I responded with "How could I ever forget about you.'"

Puzzled, Grace looked at James. "You have been here before, I gather."

"Yes, my dear, I have." James spoke softly. His mind was wandering back in time. "You requested that I let you into my past. I am opening my heart to you." James' eyes started to well up. "I have one more mission. I want you; no, I need you to be with me when I complete it."

"Mission?" Grace wanted to know. "What mission? This is our honeymoon."

"I know." James tried so hard to constrain and control his emotions. But he couldn't. He wept bitterly. He cried like a baby. He buried his head in Grace's shoulder. "I really need you to help me."

Grace's heart melted like butter. "I will. Where you go, I will go. Whatever you must do, I will do with you." James could hear her sincerity.

"I love you Grace," were the only words James could stammer.

That evening, James and Grace were invited to join the villagers in an evening of festivities. It was a celebration of the harvest moon. As dictated by custom and culture, every year this small community congregated to give thanks for the summer's bounty and to offer praise for the new season soon to come.

The celebration included food gathered from the fields, drink, and dance. James and Grace were invited to sit with the village official who, years ago, opted to save James' life. Before he and Grace could react, they were hurled into the traditional dance of gratitude. There they stood in the center for all to see.

Their bodies were pressed tightly with one another. They could feel the heartbeat of the other. The electricity exchanged between both James and Grace was evident for everyone to see. Their eyes locked onto the others. It was time. It was their time. They could feel it. It was their time to do some sowing of their own.

That evening, James and Grace became one flesh. The passion of that evening would resonate for many years to follow.

The morning's sun came too quickly. James woke up. He found his wife lying snugly against his shoulder. With her right hand resting comfortably on James chest, he could not help but notice how beautiful she was as she slept. Her face glowed as bright as the harvest moon they celebrated the night before: and it glistened as brilliantly as the sun breaking over the mountains.

Gingerly, James removed her arm from his chest. Gently shaking her, "Honey, we need to get moving." He said.

"Where are we going?" She whispered as she was still caught somewhere between her state of bliss to the breaking of the sun.

"The mission, sweetheart," James reminded her of "The mission."

"Can't it wait for another ten minutes?" She inquired.

"No, I am afraid it can't. It's going to be a long and hard day. We need to get moving."

"Okay." Grace replied. "Five more minutes, then."

James conceded: "Five more minutes."

"Thanks honey," Grace smiled.

It was no less than thirty seconds that James deceived her into believing five minutes had elapsed.

"Grace, honey," he said. "Your five minutes is up. You need to get up and we need to get moving."

"Already," she muttered. "That went quickly."

They both got dressed and started the long arduous journey down the steep hills of Honduras. Thankfully, they both were fit. Grace, however, still had no idea where they were heading or what the purpose for this particular mission. Once they made it down the steep slopes, Grace demanded they stop for a ten-minute breather.

"We don't have time. We need to keep moving." James commanded, and demanded.

"Don't treat me like a soldier!" Grace snapped. "Remember, I am your wife?"

Grace saw a side of James she never saw before. He was determined to get wherever and to whatever he needed to go.

He looked back at Grace as she came to a screeching halt. "You win!" He said smiling. "You can stay here while I finish what must be done."

"Really?" Grace said so innocently.

"Really," James said smugly. "I should be back before the sun starts to hide behind the hills. Just one thing sweetheart?"

Relieved, Grace asked: "What's that honey?"

"Watch out for the snakes. They have a way of sneaking up on a person."

James turned around and headed toward the sound of the stream. Within seconds he could hear Grace calling out to him. "James! James! You can't leave me here."

Before she knew it, she was soon behind him. She shadowed his every move, all the while looking for any signs of a snake. They walked along the stream's edge until they came to a shallow spot for them to cross.

"I am not going to cross this stream!" Grace cried out.

Knowing time was against them, James was not about to bicker with his beloved wife. He picked her up and carried her across the rushing water. She wrapped her arms around his neck. "I can get use to this," she thought.

Once they made it to the other side, there was nothing but mountain staring before them. "Let me guess," Grace said. "We are going to have to climb, aren't we?"

James found humor in her question. "Yes, yes we are. Look at the bright side," he said.

"And what is that?" Grace wondered.

"We only have to go half way up." James replied.

"Great!" she said, rolling her eyes. "What is the purpose of this mission again?" Grace truly needed to understand. She wanted to support James, but it was becoming a bit more than she bargained.

"You will see. Take my hand." Together they made the strenuous walk up the steep slopes. They got about half way when James halted. There was something eerie about this spot. It was hallowed. Grace could sense that something horrible happened there. It was evident to the eye that the ground had been disturbed at some point.

Grace observed skeletal remains buried underneath some foliage. She also could see where the trees told a tale of unspeakable pain. They cried out as they were laced and lined with traces of gunfire.

James looked her in the eyes. "This is where I need you." He babbled. "Stand here and please don't leave me." He instructed. "Like I'm going anywhere," Grace thought to herself.

Grace understood this was the past that plagued James.

James took a few steps forward. He reached down to his right ankle where he pulled out the knife he used years ago. He fell to his knees. He sobbed uncontrollably. He looked toward the sky and shouted as loud and as long as his voice would permit. "I am so, so sorry!"

He then took his knife and stabbed into the soil where his friend drew his last breath. As he thrust the knife into the earth below, Grace noticed a letter sticking from its blade. She slowly approached James. She put her hands on his shoulders to offer comfort. Her curiosity got the best of her. She had to know. She looked at the handwriting on the paper that now stood to signify a time long ago but never forgotten. It read: "It is hard for me to say I'm sorry." It was the same knife that was plunged into the wooden floor of her parent's house.

Chapter 36

"HMMM?"

A BLANKET OF SNOW COVERED Jefferson County. "I love snow for Christmas," Grace thought to herself. A strong scent of fresh pine filled the house. A continuous loop of Christmas carols played over the radio. Grace was engrossed with the Baby Jesus figure. She gave the little statue a kiss before placing Him in the manger scene.

Coming down the stairs, "She finally fell asleep," James said, referring to Rosie, as he tossed another log onto the fire. Rosie was excited about Santa and she didn't want to miss seeing him. "How did you manage that?" Grace asked. "I told her this was Santa's first visit to Rosie McIntyre's, and he might not stop if she wasn't sound asleep."

James settled onto the sofa next to his wife. The glow of the Christmas tree and the flames from the fire gave warmth to the cold Christmas Eve night. Grace loved that James worked from home now. She looked forward to the late nights in front of the glowing fire. Tonight was special. Tonight was Christmas Eve: her first Christmas as Mrs. James McIntyre.

James wrapped his arm around her as she snuggled up against his side. Her heart fluttered in thought as her mind took her back on their journey.

A little teary eyed, her memories drifted back to Ray. How things have changed. At one time long ago, Grace may have felt that her introduction to James was contrived. But after falling in love with James and marrying him, she no longer saw it as a contrived relationship, but one of fate, or a mission of God's will.

Just as a Command Sergeant sends his soldiers on a mission, so too does the Heavenly Father send His people on a mission. Ray Howard not only served his country, but he also served a higher power. The mission that Ray performed best was that of a peacekeeper. Ray's mission as assigned by the will of His Heavenly Father was to bring a life of peace to James. Ray's life was a sacrifice by the will of God that allowed James to have new life, renewed hope, and peace.

Grace nuzzled a little closer to James.

"James"

Opening his eyes, "Hmmm?"

"Next Christmas we are going to need another stocking on that mantle."

CPSIA information can be obtained
at www.ICGtesting.com
Printed in the USA
FFHW01n0040240818
48005634-51699FF